Seniors At Large

By Tim M. Dutton

Seniors At Large

Copyright © 2012 by Tim Dutton

http://warriorcombatives.com/

ISBN: 978-0-9840839-2-3

Published in the United States of America

Table of Contents

Chapter 1
A Blast From the Past

1973 - Vietnam...

Battle ravaged Field just below a heavily enemy filled hill. Explosions and gun fire can be heard all around. Numerous American Army soldiers are hunkered down in trenches returning fire. Young Joe "G.I." Cotton, a slim, muscular Army Sergeant in his early thirties with a "military style flat top", is chewing on a cigar and kneeling next to a Young, lanky Radio Operator, who is talking on the radio. The Radio Operator lowers the receiver and looks at G.I. with a worried expression on his face. "Sarge, their not sending reinforcements. We're out gunned and out manned and we're gonna die ain't we?"

G.I. calmly takes the cigar out of his mouth and looks the radio operator in the eyes. "Calm down soldier I been in worse situations than this. There is always a chance your gonna die, that's not

1

always your choice, but what is your choice is how you die. Now, would you rather go out whimpering or go out roaring?"

The radio operator starts to muster up some courage and smiles. "Roaring Sir."

G.I. smiles back and slaps the radio operator on the shoulder. "That's the spirit soldier."

G.I. repositions himself where he can address the other soldiers. "Listen up men, the situation is bad and H.Q. is not gonna send us any help, so whatever we do we're gonna do it alone."

The soldiers all look around at each other worried as G.I. continues. "I'm not gonna order you to do anything against your will, when a man faces death, he ought to be able to do so with free will."

G.I. looks at the cigar he's been holding, throws it on the ground, then looks back at the men. "You got three choices. One, you can stay in this ditch, in which case you will definitely die. Two you can retreat and hope your fast enough not to catch a bullet in the back, you likely stand a fifty, fifty chance of making it. Three you can charge that hill and show these pansies what Americans are made of. If you charge that hill you got about a twenty five percent chance of surviving, but you got a one hundred percent chance of making history and if you die, you'll die a hero."

G.I. unholsters his Colt .45, slightly pulls back

the slide to make sure a round is chambered, then re-holsters it, he takes a cigar out of his pocket, puts it in his mouth, then pulls the bolt on his rifle back to chamber a round and looks at his men. "I figure you already know what choice I'm making, and I'll be the first one out of this ditch. If your gonna lead ya gotta go first. So when your ready let's get to it."

A soldier in the distance speaks his support. "We're with you sarge. Warriors all the way let's show these sallies what real fighting men can do."

All the men in the trenches whoop and holler in excitement and determination. G.I. looks at his men and smiles big and proud. "I love this job."

Then - Joe Cotton - Professional Soldier

1978 - Bomar City, USA...

A filthy alley behind a restaurant, garbage and boxes strung all about. Young Larry "Dirty Larry" Westwood, a slim, filthy and dirty young man in his mid thirties with uncombed, matted hair, is digging in a large dumpster. Leaning against the dumpster is a handwritten, cardboard panhandling sign that reads: "*Need money, not willing to work.*" Dirty Larry raises a half eaten hamburger out of the dumpster it is covered with maggots. Dirty Larry brushes away the maggots and takes a big bite. It is visually obvious that he is enjoying the

3

burger by the expression on his face. He wipes his mouth with his dirty sleeve leaving a worse smear of filth and grime.

Then - Larry Westwood - Unemployed and Homeless

1972 - Bomar City...

In a large office building, a door leading to an office has a sign that reads: "*Cecil Poindexter, CPA*."

Frustrated, a young Cecil "Cowboy" Poindexter, a slim, nerdy looking young man in his late twenties, wearing a suit and tie, sits behind a desk crunching numbers. Cowboy places his hands behind his head, leans back in his chair and stares up at the ceiling, as though he is in deep thought. Gloria Finch, a heavy set elderly women, walks over to Cecil's desk and puts a stack of papers on the desk. "Are you daydreaming about being a cowboy again?" Mrs. Finch asks.

Slightly startled Cowboy sits up in his chair and then smiles. "Yes, ma'am, I guess you caught me."

"I brought those files you needed." Mrs. Finch says.

"Thank you, Mrs. Finch."

"Your welcome. Are you going to be at the show tomorrow?"

Cowboy looks up and smiles. "Yes ma'am I

wouldn't miss it. It's the only thing that gets me through the week anymore."

Mrs. Finch nods. "Well, I'll see you there then. If you don't need anything else I'm going to head on home."

"That will be fine, Mrs. Finch thank you again and drive carefully."

Mrs. Finch appreciates the concern her boss shows her. He has always treated her with respect and dignity. "I will, Goodnight Cecil."

Cowboy is not wearing a hat, but he pretends to tip his hat. "Goodnight ma'am."

Mrs. Finch smiles and walks out of the room. Cowboy once again places his hands behind his head, leans back in the chair and stares at the ceiling in deep thought.

Then - Cecil Poindexter - CPA (Professional Bean Counter)

1968 - Somewhere in Bomar County...

On a backwoods country road, a young Henry "Speed" Jackson, an average sized young black man in his late twenties, with a country "good ole boy" look about him, is loading cases of moonshine into the trunk of a brand new 1968 Chevy Camaro, and packing hay around it to keep it tight and in place. The Camaro is solid black with a hood scoop and heavy duty rear shocks make the back of the car set up higher than the front. The rear tires are also wider than the front. Helping load the car is Uncle Jeb, a very large, muscular, "hillbilly" looking black man in his early forties. "This here's the best rot gut I've ever made, ya best be careful with it, boy,. Don't break it and don't get caught." Uncle Jeb says.

Speed gives him a kind of cockeyed look. "I ain't lost a bottle yet Uncle Jeb."

Speed pats the 68 Camaro. "And with this baby here, I reckon I'm gonna be mighty hard ta catch."

Uncle Jeb lets out a chuckle that doesn't make a sound, but shakes his whole body. "I reckon your right. You just do what you do and get this shine over to Rufus in Boon County."

Later...

Speed is driving down a country road, he looks in the rear view mirror and sees Sheriff Deputies chasing him in patrol cars. Speed grins real big, steps on the gas and pats the dash with his hand. "Let's see what you can do baby. Whoo hoo, catch me if ya can deputy Doolittle."

There are four patrol cars chasing speed. Speed does a power-slide and stops sideways in the middle of the dirt road. The patrol cars slide to a stop trying to avoid a collision, the fourth patrol car slams into the back of the third. The lead deputy picks up his radio's microphone, flips a switch and gives Speed an order over the loud speaker. "Shut off the engine and step out of the vehicle."

Speed guns it, spinning dirt out from the rear tires and starts doing donuts in the road, throwing up a cloud of dust. Then he takes off, straight off the road picking up speed and heading for a river. The deputies continue the pursuit, but as Speed gets closer to the river you can here the Lead Deputy on the radio. "This guys a lunatic. all deputies stop, stop your cars."

The patrol cars stop, at the same moment Speed hits an embankment and flies over the river, as he's going over the river you can hear him from the car. "Whooo hoo hoo hooo."

Speed's 68 Camaro lands on the other side of the river and slides sideways and stops. Speed leans out the window and waves to the deputies, then guns it again making his escape.

Then - Henry Jackson - Professional Bootlegger

1972 - outskirts of the town of Boon...

At a construction site for a new housing edition, a young Dale "Mr. Fix-it" SPENCER, a young man in his mid thirties with an average build and height, wearing a tool belt, is sawing three porch posts off using a handsaw. He saws all three off rapidly back to back, then grabs all three posts and

7

slings them over his shoulder and carries them over to a porch and drops them on the ground.

There are Two other workers on the porch waiting to install the post. Jeremiah is a thin, elderly black man. Drew is a brawny looking, young white boy. Mr. Fix-it sets a post in it's place by Jeremiah, it's a perfect fit, Jeremiah smiles and watches as Mr. Fix-it sets another post in place by Drew, it too is a perfect fit. Drew starts to nail the post in place. Jeremiah shakes his head in amazement. Mr. Fix-it stands the last post up on the end, which is also a perfect fit, and starts nailing it in place. Jeremiah chuckles and smiles. "You just look at a space once, then you go cut a perfect fit every time. How in tarnation do you do that, Dale?"

Mr. Fix-it looks up at Jeremiah, smiles and points to his own eye. "It's all in the eyes sir."

Then - Dale Spencer - Professional Carpenter

1968 - Bomar City...

The Red Light District, a seedy looking part of town with various "criminal types" loitering about. Margret "Lady Po Po" Jefferson, a very attractive black vice cop in her early twenties, wearing heavy make-up and dressed like a prostitute, is leaning in the passenger side window of a stopped car next to the curb. Down the street a man's voice can be heard yelling and getting closer. "Stop, police, stop, your under arrest, stop."

Lady Po Po raises up and looks down the sidewalk to see a biker, a burly, mean looking man wearing a leather vest and tattoos all over his arms, running toward her. He is being chased by Phil Booth, a rookie cop in his early twenties with an average build. Phil is starting to get out of breath. When the biker reaches Lady Po Po's position he stops turns around, pulls a gun out of his waist band and aims it at Phil. Phil shocked, freezes in position and is unable to move. "I'm not going back to prison, pig." The biker says.

Lady Po Po kicks the gun out of Bikers hand, hits him with a right cross to the face, grabs his arm, shoulder throws him to the ground, puts her foot on his neck, then pulls a small gun and a badge out of her purse and points both at the biker. "Freeze scum bag. I believe your wrong about going back to prison and you better be glad you didn't kill a cop or things could have went a lot worse."

Phil calms down and approaches Lady Po Po's position. "You okay officer?" Lady Po Po asks.

"Yes ma'am, thank you." Phil answers.

Lady Po Po smiles. "Your welcome. You must be new I haven't seen you around before. Whats your name?"

"Phil Booth ma'am. This is my second week.

You saved my life, if you ever need anything you just ask and I mean anything, I owe you big time."

Lady Po Po winks. "I may take you up on that one of these days Phil. I'm Margret Jefferson with vice and it's good to meet you. Why don't you call this in and we can get this scum bag taken care of."

Then - Margret Jefferson - Professional Vice Cop

1983 - outskirts of Bomar City...

Grace "Super Granny" Hudson, a friendly looking "granny type" in her mid forties, is standing out by the street in front of a two-story house. A large sign in the front yard reads: "*Second Chance Home*" in large letters and under that in smaller letters it reads: "*Home for troubled teens - all are welcomed with open arms and an open heart.*"

There are several teenagers in front of the house playing volleyball, they all stop to look when a police patrol car pulls up to the curb in front of the house and stops. Sam Bennett, an experienced looking Police Sergeant in his mid forties, gets out of the drivers side of the patrol car and walks around to Super Granny. Phil Booth, now an average built officer in his mid thirties, gets out of the passengers side and stands next to Sam. "Hello Mrs. Hudson. We have another one for you, his name is Danny Thompson and he has no family so he may be with you for awhile." Sam says.

"I know Sam, social services gave me the heads up."

Super Granny looks at Phil and smiles. "I don't believe I've met you yet young man?"

Sam pats his partner on the back. "This is Phil Booth, he's my new partner, Bob retired last week. Phil this is Grace Hudson, she runs this place."

Phil nods to Super Granny. "Glad to meet you, ma'am."

Super Granny nods back with a warm smile. "It's a pleasure to meet you too Phil."

Super Granny winks at Phil. "You couldn't have asked for a better partner than old Sam here."

Sam, slightly embarrassed ducks his head. "Thanks, Grace."

Super Granny smiles at Sam, then looks at the rear door of the patrol car. "Well, I believe we better let the young man out."

Phil looks at Sam, who nods his head, Phil opens the door. Danny Thompson (Later Hudson), a scrawny boy in his mid teens, steps out of the patrol car, his hands are handcuffed in the front and he has ankle cuffs on his ankles.

Super Granny looks at the ankle cuffs and frowns. "I know the handcuffs are standard procedure, but what's with the leg irons?"

"He's a runner Grace." Sam says.

Super Granny looks at Sam and pretends to be confused. "You put leg irons on people because they like to run a little?"

"No, I mean he tries to escape." Sam says

Super Granny looks at Sam and smiles. "I know what you meant Sam I was just foolin'."

Sam a little embarrassed smiles, ducks his head and nods. Super Granny turns her attention back to Danny. "Well, I can't keep him hobbled up like that around here so you might as well take em' off now."

Phil looks at Sam who once again nods, Phil removes the handcuffs and puts them away then bends down and removes the ankle cuffs and hands them to Sam. Danny rubs his wrist, looks at the officers, then at Super Granny, smiles and bolts across the yard. Super Granny takes off after him. Phil starts to join the chase, but before he can get going Sam grabs him by the shoulder and stops him. Sam nods his head up as though to silently say "watch". Phil stops and watches the chase between Super Granny and Danny.

Danny runs at full speed toward a fence when he approaches it he slows down to put both hands on the fence and then side vaults over it. Super Granny never slows down and is able to close the gap by jumping the fence at full speed, she grabs Danny by the shoulder to stop him. Danny spins around and swings a punch at her. Super Granny blocks the punch and rolls her arm around Danny's arm to lock it out, she then drops him to the ground on his back with his arm still locked out.

Back at the patrol car...

Sam is smiling and enjoying the show. Phil is shocked and amazed as he sees Super Granny in action, eyes wide he looks at Sam. "What is she, some kind of Super Granny?"

Sam, still smiling looks at Phil and nods. "That she is. I believe that name fits her to a tee."

The other side of the fence...

Super Granny is still holding Danny on the ground in an arm bar. "Now are you going to calm down?"

"Yes ma'am and I'm sorry I ran from ya."

Super Granny relaxes and releases her hold on Danny's arm, Danny sits up next to her. Super Granny puts her arm around Danny's shoulder. "This place is not an orphanage or a prison, it can be your home if you give it a chance. If your going to live here your gonna have to act accordingly."

Danny is nodding in agreement the whole time Super Granny is talking. "We don't run away from our problems, we face them. We don't put our hands on someone without their permission and we treat each other with respect. Now, do you understand and think you want to give it try?"

13

Danny nods. "Yes ma'am, I want to try."

Super Granny smiles. "Good. Now let's go see if the other kids left some cookies for you to eat."

Then - Grace Hudson - Manager of Home for Troubled Teens

1968 - outskirts of the town of Boon...

An average looking "country type" County fair, a large banner over the entrance reads: "*Boon County Fair.*" There are lots of different people roaming about including men, women and children.

A "wrestling/boxing type" ring is situated at one edge of the fair, with spectator seats in front and to the sides. Three "red necks" are sitting in the front row waiting for the show to start. Bubba, a large, muscular man in his mid twenties, is barefoot and wearing faded overalls with no shirt, he has a big dip of snuff in his lip, it's so big he can barely close his mouth. Skeeter, a scrawny, bucktoothed man in his early twenties, is also wearing faded overalls, but his are at least three sizes to big, he is also wearing an old worn out pair of lace-up work boots that are also to big. Muley, a large, obese, man in his late twenties, is wearing worn out blue jeans, a white "wife beater type" tank top that is way to small and is covered in stains, he is also wearing cowboy boots with his jean legs tucked inside.

Rose "Wild Rose" Gibson, a very attractive, petite , but athletic type young women in her mid twenties, is standing in the middle of the ring, swinging her arms and hopping from foot to foot to warm up. The Ring Announcer, a tall, lanky man in his late thirties, is standing at the edge of the ring with a megaphone addressing the crowd. "Ladies and gentlemen I have a special challenge for you today. I will give a crisp one hundred dollar bill to anyone that can stay in this ring for three minutes against wild rose. Do I have any takers?"

"Golly, that's a lot a' money." Skeeter says.

Bubba stands up and spits tobacco juice on the ground. "I'll take ya up on that offer."

The Ring Announcer looks out of the ring and sees Bubba standing near by. "Well then sir step right up and get in the ring with Wild Rose."

Bubba walks to the ring and steps in as his buddies cheer him on. "Go get her Bubba, show her why a woman shouldn't be in that ring." Skeeter says.

"Yea doggies, ya beat her like ya beat yore wife." Muley says.

Bubba and Wild Rose stand in the middle of the ring and square off against each other. Bubba points his finger at Wild Rose. "Don't think I'm gonna go easy on ya little Missy, just cause yore a little thang. My wife ain't much bigger than you and I broke her jaw last week for talkin' back, I ain't gonna take no sass from no female. We gotta get rough with y'all gals ta keep ya in yore place."

Wild rose doesn't say a word she just gives the red neck a mean look and prepares to go to work. The Ring Announcer steps out of the ring. "Now there ain't no rules, so you both just do whatever it takes to win. Are ya both ready to go?"

Both competitors nod their heads and prepare to fight. The Ring Announcer continues. "Let's get ready for a brawl. On my mark now, one...two...three fight."

Bubba quickly lunges at Wild Rose and throws a powerful right hook. Wild Rose ducks under the punch with great speed, grace and little effort. Angered, Bubba throws four rapid Hooks as hard as he can, right, left, right and left. Wild Rose ducks all four hooks just as easily as she did the first.

Now completely infuriated and out of control, Bubba rares back for a powerful right "hay-maker type" hook, and unleashes it toward Wild Rose. Wild Rose steps in and shifts all of her weight to double forearm block the strike. She then immediately slams a right back-fist into Bubba's jaw. Bubba stunned, staggers backward, Wild Rose advances and throws two powerful hooks of her own, a right hook and a left hook. Bubba's head snaps to the side with each strike and he staggers barely able to stand.

Wild Rose drops to her right knee and slams her right forearm up into Bubba's groin. Bubba makes a painful face, grabs his groin and leans forward. Wild Rose picks him up into a fireman's carry spins twice, then with one great heave, bends her knees and power lifts him over her head with arms extended.

Wild Rose, holding Bubba over her head walks to the front of the ring and throws him into the laps of his two red neck buddies. The chairs the red necks are sitting on collapse under the force and all wind up on the ground. Wild Rose leans over the top rope and points at the red necks. "Ya best not be starting fights with girls, boy, cause ya ain't man enough ta finish em'."

Then - Rose Gibson - Professional Wrestler

Chapter 2
Present State of Mind

Present day - Bomar City...

Pine Ridge Nursing Home is a large, white washed building that resembles a hospital. A large sign out front reads: "*Pine Ridge Nursing Home*" in large letters, under this in smaller letters it reads: "*Your loved one's last stay during their last days.*"

Inside...

G.I.'s room is an average looking nursing home room with the exception of military awards hanging on the walls. An older G.I. is now in his mid seventies, but is still muscular, he has the same "military style flat top" but it is now gray. G.I. is doing push-ups beside his bed and counting each one as he reaches the top of the movement. "Fifty-eight....fifty-nine....and sixty."

After the last push-up G.I. stands to his feet, grabs a towel off the bed and starts wiping sweat from his torso. Biff Buford, a heavy set, ex-Marine male orderly in his late twenties sporting a "Marine style buzz cut", walks down the hall toward G.I.'s room. Most Marines would consider it disrespectful to use the term Marine to describe Biff. Truth be told a bullet casing brushed up against Biff's arm during boot camp and his Drill Instructor used it as an opportunity to discharge him to get him out of his hair and to prevent Biff from disgracing the Marine Corps. Biff stands in the door way of G.I.'s room. "Why don't you hang it up old man? Your to old to do anything anyway."

G.I. turns and looks at Biff with a *tough as nails look on his face*. "I'm still young enough to go toe-to-toe with you Jar Head. Anytime you want to throw down you just say the word and we'll go."

Biff is not sure how to respond, G.I. grabs a cigar off of the night stand and puts it in his mouth. "You don't have a right to talk anyhow. This country is at war and here you are a young man claiming to be a Marine and your pushing adult diapers around. Your a disgrace to the real Marines out there putting their lives on the line. So ya need ta keep your mouth shut ya little Daisy May."

Biff pulls up his shirt sleeve to reveal a small band-aid. "I got a medical discharge and besides your not supposed to have cigars in here."

G.I. chomps down on the cigar and takes a step

forward. "Why don't you come and take it then, Daisy May."

Biff gets a shocked look on his face. "You crazy old man."

Biff turns and angrily stomps off. G.I. shakes his head in disgust. "Out of all the nursing homes I could have went to, I get sent to the one that has a smart mouthed, wanna be jar head."

Now - Joe Cotton - AKA - G.I. - Retired

Nursing home bathing area...

An elderly Dirty Larry, a slim, filthy and dirty elderly man in his late sixties with uncombed, matted gray hair, is being held in the air by Two Male orderlies trying to get Dirty Larry into the bathtub. One of the orderlies is Biff Buford, the other is Jack Longbow, a big, burly, American Indian male orderly. The orderlies struggle to get Dirty Larry into the tub, but Dirty Larry is struggling every step of the way. "Come on Larry, you gotta take your bath." Jack says.

"No, it's not been a year yet, I take a bath once a year, no more. Even once a year is optional, now let me down." Dirty Larry says.

The orderlies manage to get Dirty Larry into the tub, but he is still squirming and struggling to get out. Both orderlies are getting sopping wet from splashed water as they try to hold Dirty Larry in the tub. "We do this every time. I'm glad we don't try to give him a bath more than once a month." Biff says.

Dirty Larry Struggles a little harder. "I knew it, it's only been a month, not a year, now let me out of here."

Jack pats Dirty Larry on the shoulder. "Calm down Larry, we're just trying to do our jobs. The quicker you calm down, the quicker we can get this over with."

With a disappointed look on his face, Dirty Larry stops struggling and submits to the bath. As the orderlies start to clean him up, Dirty Larry's eyes widen and he smiles, then bubbles come up out of the water. Jack leans backward and pinches his nose."Oh, not again. Do you have to do that every time?"

Biff gets a whiff and quickly covers his mouth and nose with his hand and rushes to the toilet, sticks his head in and starts heaving and gagging. Jack shakes his head in disgust. "My god. How can that smell that bad?"

Dirty Larry shrugs. "That's what you people feed us in here, it don't smell much better when we eat it."

Biff seems to get control and raises his head out of the toilet. Dirty Larry sits up straight and smiles big. "Here comes another one."

Biff's head goes back into the toilet as he once

again begins to heave and gag. Jack continues to shake his head in disgust. Dirty Larry, enjoying himself, smiles even bigger.

Now - Larry Westwood - AKA - Dirty Larry - Ward of the State

Nursing home lounge...

Cowboy, a now slim, nerdy looking elderly man in his late sixties and wearing a cowboy hat, is sitting at a bench excitedly telling a story to Two other nursing home patients. Mr. Crawford, is a heavy set elderly man with a cranky look about him. Mr. Dunn, is a skinny elderly man with no teeth. By the looks on their faces, you can tell that neither of them believes a word that Cowboy is telling them.

Cowboy cannot contain his excitement as he tells his story. "Then I jumped up onto the back of my horse, so that I'm standing while the horse is still running, then I pull both revolvers and fire off twelve shots, every bullet hits it's mark and...."

"Excuse me, Mr. Poindexter I need to interrupt you for a minute, I'm in a Hurry."

Cowboy turns to see Nurse Ratchet, a heavy set nurse with a mean look, approaching him with a folder in her hand. As soon as Cowboy turns his head the two Residents quickly get up and walk away. "Mr. Poindexter can you check over these

23

financial reports and make sure their right?" Asks Nurse Ratchet.

Cowboy starts to object. "Well, I..."

"That will be great, thank you so much."

Nurse Ratchet hands Cowboy the folder and quickly walks away. Cowboy turns back to see his listeners have abandoned him, he ducks his head in disappointment.

Now - Cecil Poindexter - AKA - Cowboy - Retired?

Nursing home hall way...

Speed, now an average sized elderly black man in his early seventies and still has that "good ole boy" look about him, is riding on a gurney as it speeds down the hall. Jack and Biff are running after him. Nurses and orderlies are diving out of the way to keep themselves from being run down. The gurney wheels are rattling because it's going so fast and Speed is thoroughly enjoying the ride. "Stop speed your going to kill someone." Jack says.

Speed pays him no mind, he's enjoying the ride. "Whooo hoo hoo hoooo."

Now - Henry Jackson - AKA - Speed - Retired

Nursing home lounge...

Mr. Fix-it, now an elderly man in his mid

seventies with average build and height, always wearing a tool belt, is sitting at a table. He wiggles the table and notices that it is wobbly, so he stands up, the tables height comes to about his waist. He turns the table over and measures the legs with a tape measure he gets real close and squints to see the measurement, then makes a mark on one leg with a pencil. He marks another leg the same way, then once more in the same manner marks the third leg of the table. Mr. Fix-it pulls a small hand saw out of his tool belt and starts sawing on one of the table legs.

Later...

The table is back in an upright position, its height now comes to his thighs. Mr. Fix-it wiggles it again and it still wobbles, he shrugs his shoulders and pulls the small saw back out.

Later...

The table now comes to Mr. Fix-it's knees and it still wobbles. He scratches his head in confusion and once again pulls the small saw out.

Later...

The tables height now only comes to Mr. Fix-its ankles, he wiggles it and it still wobbles, he folds his arms and shakes his head in frustration. Mr. Crawford and Mr. Dunn are sitting at a bench seat near the window, watching Mr. Fix-it work on the table. "Does he know what he's doing?" Mr. Crawford asks.

Mr. Dunn shrugs. "He already cut it off three times and it's still to short."

Mr. Crawford points to Mr. Fix-it. "Did ya see the way he squinted to read that measuring thingy."

Mr. Dunn nods. "Yea, I think he's blind in one eye and can't see out of the other."

Mr. Fix-it is still standing at the table with his arms folded and a frustrated look on his face.

Now - Dale Spencer - AKA - Mr. Fix-it - Retired

Nursing home cafeteria...

Lady Po Po, now an elderly, heavy set black woman in her late sixties still wearing heavy make-up and dressed like a prostitute, is leaning against a cafeteria table talking to Mr. Crawford and Mr. Dunn. Another resident, Mr. Spry, a very skinny, elderly man in his late eighties, with uncombed, thinning, gray hair in a wheelchair, rolls by. "Looking good Lady Po Po. If I was forty years younger I'd take a chance on going to jail just for one date with you."

Lady Po Po turns and smiles at Mr. Spry. "Oh you old flirt, you say the sweetest things."

Mr. Spry winks at Lady Po Po and keeps on rolling by without taking his eyes off her. A big, rough looking, Burly Man in his mid thirties with tattoos all over his body, long hair and a scraggly beard, is sitting at another table with various other people, he appears to be in a very bad mood. Mr. Spry is so preoccupied with Lady Po Po that he doesn't see the Burly Man and bumps into him with his wheelchair. The Burly Man, angry, stands up, puts his foot on the wheelchair and pushes it backward with a hard kick. Mr. Spry rolls back into another table. "You best watch where your going old man." The Burly Man says.

Mr. Spry is old enough that not much scares him anymore. Like a Banty rooster he's willing to take on all comers. "You best keep your feet to yourself, before I whoop your sissified, hippie butt. I'd already done it, but I don't hit girls and I can't tell what you are with that long hair."

The Burly Man, now infuriated, stomps toward Mr. Spry, pointing his index finger at him as he approaches. "I don't care how old you are you old codger, I'm gonna knock those false teeth right out of that smart mouth of yours."

Before the Burly Man can reach Mr. Spry, Lady Po Po grabs his finger, twists his arm behind his back, slams him against the table and torques up on his arm for a pain compliance hold. "You better learn how to respect your elders young man, before you get yourself hurt."

Lady Po Po torques up on his arm a little harder.

"Now, are you gonna calm down and go back to your own business?"

The Burly Man cringes in pain as he answers. "Ye..yes ma'am."

Now - Margret Jefferson - AKA - Lady Po Po - Retired

Nursing home hallway...

Super Granny, now an elderly woman in her early seventies with the same "granny" look about her, is walking down the hall. Jack Longbow walks out of a room as she passes by, he walks up behind her and puts his hand on her shoulder. "Good morning Mrs. Hudson."

Super Granny out of reflex wraps her arm around Jack's arm and locks it up. Jack in mild pain raises to his tippy-toes and is unable to move. Super Granny realizes who it is and lets him go and puts her hand on his shoulder. "I'm sorry Jack it was a force of habit. You really shouldn't sneak up on somebody and put your hands on them."

"Yes ma'am I should have let you know I was there, I'm sorry, I won't do it again."

Super Granny smiles warm and friendly. "That's okay, now if your alright how about we go to the cafeteria and see if we can find you some cookies."

NOW - Grace Hudson - AKA - Super Granny - Retired

Wild Rose's room...

Wild Rose, now a petite , but athletic type elderly women in her late sixties, is sleeping in her bed. Jack opens the door and walks over to the bed holding a needle in one hand, with the other hand he shakes Wild Rose to wake her. "Wake up Rose. Rose? Rose wake up."

Startled Wild Rose quickly sets up in bed. "What? What is it?"

"I gotta give you a shot Ms. Gibson."

Wild Rose now agitated gets out of bed and stands to talk to Jack. "A shot? What for?"

"It's ta help you sleep."

Wild Rose is now getting angry. "What do ya mean help me sleep? You woke me up ta give me a shot ta help me sleep? Don't ya have any common sense a' tawl?"

"It's on your chart, now calm down and take your shot." Jack says.

With his free hand Jack grabs Wild Rose and tries to turn her around so he can give her a shot. Wild Rose knocks his hand away, then knocks the needle out of his other hand, she grabs both his shoulders and quickly spins him around, wraps her arms around his neck and puts him in a *sleeper hold*. "Wake me up to give me a shot ta help me sleep. This here will help you sleep."

Jack quickly fades off to dreamland, Wild Rose

gently lays him on the floor and crawls back in bed to sleep.

Now - Rose Gibson - AKA - Wild Rose – Retired

Chapter 3
Pills, Pride and Plans

Nursing home lounge...

Cowboy is sitting at a table, talking to an elderly woman. The woman he is talking to is, Marge, an average sized woman in her mid sixties who is a little quirky. Marge is finishing up knitting on an item that looks like a long rope, she wraps it around Cowboys neck like a scarf, but has to keep wrapping to take up the slack. "I made this scarf for you, to keep you warm on those cold nights."

Marge finally gets the *scarf* wrapped around Cowboy's neck, he can't hardly move his head, because so much is wrapped around it. "There don't you feel warmer already?" Marge asks.

Cowboy is confused and not quite sure how to respond. "Um, yea it's, um great. You really shouldn't have gone to all the trouble."

"Nothing is to much trouble for you, Cowboy."

Marge flirtatiously bats her eyes at Cowboy. Cowboy hesitantly smiles back at her. "Um, thanks Marge."

Marge smiles and continues to bat her eyes.

At another table...

Super Granny is sitting at the table reading to her grandson. Jimmy Hudson, Super Granny's grand son, a heavy set little boy around six years old, is Danny's son. Danny Hudson (formerly Thompson) was the young man brought to Super Granny back in 1983. Super Granny adopted him and raised him as her own, now he has a son that thinks the sun rises and sets with Super Granny. Jimmy is holding a super hero action figure and listening intently as Super Granny reads. Nurse Ratchet walks over and places a cup of pills and a glass of water on the table. "Here's your afternoon pills Grace."

Nurse Ratchet continues on, distributing pills to other residents. Super Granny starts taking the pills and has a hard time swallowing each one. Jimmy watches as Super Granny appears to have a hard time taking all of the pills. Super granny gulps down the last pill and appears to be slightly out of breath. "How come you gotta take so many pills Granny?" Jimmy asks.

"So that they will make me feel better." Super Granny answers.

"So do you feel better after you take them?" Jimmy asks.

Super Granny looks up as though she is in heavy thought, as she ponders the question her grandson just asked.

Later that night...

In her room, Super Granny is sitting in front of a mirror brushing her hair when she hears a knock at the door, she turns to see, Nurse Ratchet opening the door. Nurse Ratchet puts another cup of pills and a glass of water on a small table next to the door. "Here's your evening pills Grace."

Nurse Ratchet closes the door back as she leaves. Super Granny gets up and walks over to the table and picks up the glass of water and one pill. She raises the pill toward her mouth, but stops before she puts it in, she looks up in thought once more thinking about what her grandson asked. In her mind she can hear his voice. "How come you gotta take so many pills Granny? So do they make you feel better after you take them?"

Super Granny looks at the pill in her hand, puts it back in the cup and throws the whole cup of pills in a near by trash bucket. "They don't make me feel any better, in fact since I started taking them I feel weak and groggy."

The next morning...

Super Granny gets out of bed, does a double biceps pose, then swings her arms back and forth. She does a few squats, then raises the end of the bed up off the floor and puts it back down. Super Granny smiles and nods her head. "I feel better already."

Super Granny hears a knock on the door and turns to see, Nurse Ratchet opening the door. Nurse Ratchet puts another cup of pills and a glass of water on the small table. "Here's your morning pills Grace."

Nurse Ratchet closes the door behind herself as she leaves. Without any hesitation, Super Granny grabs the pills and throws them in the trash bucket and smiles.

Nursing home lounge...

The lounge is full of residents including, the "Senior Gang" which includes: Super Granny, Speed, G.I., Lady Po Po, Dirty Larry, Mr. Fix-it, Wild Rose and Cowboy. Super Granny walks over to the table she was sitting at with her grandson and sees his action figure on the table, she picks it up, looks at it and smiles. An angry Nurse Ratchet stomps in and approaches Super Granny. Nurse Ratchet slams two cups of pills down on the table. "Whats this? We found these in your trash can. You think you can stop taking your pills whenever you want to?"

Super Granny looks Nurse Ratchet in the eyes. "Yes I can, it's my body and you can't force me to take anything I don't want to take."

Nurse Ratchet gets a smug grin on her face. "Oh yea? We'll see about that."

Nurse Ratchet grabs a pill and tries to force it into Super Granny's mouth. Super Granny knocks the pill out of Nurse Ratchet's hand and pushes her away. Nurse Ratchet staggers back with a shocked look on her face, stunned at Super Granny's new found strength. Super Granny knocks the pills off the table and sends them flying across the room. "I'm not gonna be forced to take those mind controlling pills ever again."

On the other side of the lounge, Mr. Crawford and Mr. Dunn watch the pills hit the wall and scatter on the floor, they both look at each other with surprised looks. "Pills, we gotta get the pills." They both say at the same time.

Mr. Crawford, Mr. Dunn and several other residents scramble to get the pills as fast as they can, which is not very fast, it's a very slow race to get the pills. Mr. Wang, an average built elderly man who uses a walker to get around, is last, He moves the walker forward, then slides his feet forward, he continues these motions as fast has he can while he is very excited. "Is there any little blue pills? Save me the blue pills. I need the blue pills."

Super Granny looks at the action figure in her hand and gets a determined look on her face. Super Granny does a back handspring away from Nurse Ratchet, then stares defiantly at her. Super Granny grabs the front of her own blouse and rips it open to reveal a tee-shirt with big letters that read, "*SG*".

Nurse Ratchet Now scowling, snaps her fingers. Biff comes into the lounge and stands behind Nurse Ratchet, with his arms folded across his chest. Jack comes in behind Biff and stands beside him with his arms also crossed. Lou, A big orderly with a bodybuilders physique, comes in and stands beside Biff and Jack. "If you want to do it the hard way, we'll do it the hard way." Nurse Ratchet says.

The rest of the Senior Gang gather behind Super Granny, with their arms folded across their chests. "We got your back, Super Granny." Cowboy says.

G.I. nods his head toward Biff. "Daisy May there is mine."

Biff starts to shake, then runs away screaming like a little girl. Wild Rose pounds one of her hands with her fist. "I got sleeping beauty."

Jack quickly turns and runs after Biff. "Wait for me Biff."

Lou looks at the Senior Gang, then looks around to see that Biff and Jack are gone, he quickly runs away, bumping into chairs and tables, because he's in such a hurry to get out. Nurse

Ratchet turns her head to see that the orderlies are gone, then looks back at Super Granny. "Fine, you win this time, but don't get used to it."

Nurse Ratchet stomps back out of the room. The Senior Gang high five each other. "It's time we stop letting these people disrespect us and poison us with all those pills, as much as they give us there's no way they can monitor all of the side effects." Super Granny says.

G.I. Takes a cigar out of his pocket and puts it in his mouth. "I agree with Super Granny and I also think it's time we get out of this rat hole."

Super Granny looks around at the other members of the Senior Gang. "Does everyone agree we should get out of here?"

The Senior Gang look around at each other and all nod their heads in agreement. Super Granny cautiously looks around and leans in close to the group and whispers. "Good, let's meet in the storage room at the end of the north hall and make our plans."

Nursing home storage room...

An average sized storage room with shelves on all the walls that contain canned food and other items. The Senior Gang are all huddled together discussing their escape plans. Mr. Fix-it grabs a large can off of the shelf and holds it close to his face while squinting.

37

Mr. Fix-it's point of view...

The lettering on the can appears to read: "*Grade 'A' Whoop Butt.*"

Actual point of view...

The lettering on the can actually reads: "*Grade 'A' Whipped Butter.*" Mr. Fix-it shows the can to the rest of the group."We could open up a can of this on them."

Mr. Fix-it hands the can to Super Granny. Super Granny looks at the can and with a confused look on her face, then looks at Mr. Fix-it. "Um, okay we'll do that Mr. Fix-it."

Dirty Larry steps behind Mr. Fix-it and twirls his finger at his own head and rolls his eyes in the *he's crazy* gesture. Super Granny shakes her head and puts the can on a shelf behind her. "If I had my horse, I'd have done rode out a' here with guns blazing." Cowboy says.

Super Granny looks at Cowboy with another confused look on her face. She's starting to think her friends have already taken to many of those pills. "I thought you were an accountant Cowboy?" Super Granny asks.

Cowboy nods. "Yes ma'am, I was."

Dirty Larry steps behind Cowboy and does the same *he's crazy* gesture. Super Granny once again shakes her head. Cowboy turns around to see what

Dirty Larry is doing. Dirty Larry quickly sticks his finger into his own ear, before Cowboy can see what he's doing, then innocently looks around. Dirty Larry takes his finger out of his ear and there is a big glop of ear wax stuck to the end of it. He smells the ear wax and shakes it off. Everyone makes a *yuck* face and tries to move away to avoid being hit by the ear wax glob, as it flies by and sticks to the wall.

Super Granny shakes her head again. "Okay, that's enough lolly gagging, lets get back to business. Does everyone agree we get up early first thing in the morning and make our break for it?"

Everyone looks at each other and nod in agreement. "Good. Does everyone know what your supposed to do?" Super Granny asks.

Once again everyone nods yes. Super Granny smiles, confident that they have their plan worked out. "That's the plan then and remember once we get out we're all going to meet at the park. Oh! One other thing you all need to stop taking your pills, we need clear heads if we're gonna pull this off. So no more pills."

G.I. takes a cigar out of his mouth and sticks it in his pocket. "I already stopped taking mine, I've been putting them in Nurse Ratchet's coffee."

Nurse's station...
An average looking nurse's station with a

counter and computer situated at the intersection of halls. Nurse Ogle, a short petite nurse in her mid twenties wearing *pop-bottle* style glasses that make her eyes look huge, is standing in front of the counter reading a chart. Nurse Ratchet walks up holding her stomach and looking sick. "Oh, Nurse Ogle I don't feel so good."

"Nurse Ratchet whats wrong?"

Nurse Ogle helps Nurse Ratchet to a Chair. Nurse Ratchet describes her ailments. "I have stomach cramps, my hairs coming out, my vision is blurred, I'm having hot flashes and I have a ringing in my ears."

Nurse Ogle hands Nurse Ratchet a cup of coffee and pats her on the back, she then looks at a posting on the wall, the letters that can be seen read: "*Possible side affects of resident's medication.*" under this is a very long list of side effects. Nurse Ogle places her hand over her mouth in shock and turns back to Nurse Ratchet. Nurse Ratchet, still puny looking, is sipping her coffee. "You know those symptoms sound like the side effects of medication." Nurse Ogle says.

Nurse Ratchet responds in a whiny voice. "I'm not on medication. The only way it could be side effects is if one of the residents has been slipping me their medication and I don't know how they could have done that."

Nurse Ratchet takes another sip of coffee. At

the same time Nurse Ratchet and Nurse Ogle notice and look at the coffee cup in Nurse Ratchet's hands. Nurse Ratchet Spits the coffee out on the floor and drops the cup. Nurse Ratchet becomes frantic. "I've been poisoned."

Nurse Ogle tries to console her. Nurse Ratchet's face starts to twitch and she is making all kinds of funny faces. Her next statement is slurred. "Now I can't feel my face. Whats happening to me?"

Nurse Ratchet grabs her stomach again and gets a worried look on her face. "Do you need to go to the bathroom?" Nurse Ogle asks.

Nurse Ratchet's eyes open wide in surprise, then she starts to cry. "I just did."

Chapter 4
The Escape

The next morning...

The Senior Gang is sneaking along a wall in the lobby. Jack is walking near the edge of the wall whistling. As Jack approaches the Senior Gang's position, Wild Rose jumps out behind him and puts him in a *sleeper hold*. Jack struggles to free himself, but quickly loses consciousness. Wild Rose gently lays him down on the floor. Biff comes out of a room carrying towels and sees rose standing over Jack. "Hey, whats going on here?"

G.I. jumps towards Biff and growls. "Grrrrr."

Biff, startled, throws the towels in the air and takes off running down the hall, once again screaming like a little girl. Lou comes out of the office to see whats going on. "Whats all the commotion out here?"

Cowboy maneuvers himself behind Lou with the *scarf* that Marge made him in his hands.

Cowboy Twirls the scarf over his head and lassos Lou, then quickly runs up and pulls Lou's feet out from under him. Lou falls to the ground and is laying face down on his belly. Cowboy quickly *hogties* Lou like a steer and raises his hands in the air like he was at a rodeo.

Lou struggles to get free. "Hey! Let me go. Untie me. Come on guys, this ain't funny. You better let me go before I get angry, you wouldn't like me when I'm angry. Guys? Guys? Guys?"

The Senior Gang look around to make sure it's clear and they all bolt for the front door.

Bomar City park...

The park is an average size park with walking trails and park benches. The Senior Gang is standing near an area with a bench and a water fountain. We can hear dogs barking and someone yelling in the back ground and getting closer. "Stop, stop, whats gotten into you."

The Senior Gang all look in the direction of the barking and yelling and see, a young dog walker, a plump teen-aged girl in her early teens with braces and pig tails, coming towards them, she is being pulled by a dozen dogs of different shape, size and breed. The dogs jump on Dirty Larry, knocking him to the ground. The dogs then roll on him, as though they were rolling in something dead or smelly. "Stop it, get off of him." The dog walker says.

The dog walker looks at the Senior Gang and ducks her head in embarrassment. "I'm so sorry, I don't know what's wrong with them, they've never done this to a person before."

Super Granny steps over to the dog walker to calm and console her. "It's okay sweetie we understand exactly what's going on and it's not your fault at all."

Super Granny as well as the rest of the gang know that the dogs are attracted to the smell of Dirty Larry. Dirty Larry is rolling around on the ground trying to push the dogs off. "Hey! Get off of me, help, don't just stand there help me up."

The rest of the Senior Gang try to control their laughter, but do a very poor job of it.

Later...

The Senior Gang are standing together discussing their plans. G.I. looks around to spot the water fountain and the bench, he walks over to the bench, pulls a handkerchief from his pocket and lays it on the bench, he then pulls his bottom false teeth plate out and lays it on the handkerchief. G.I. walks over to the water fountain and starts to rinse his mouth, as he does, a very obese woman, wearing a flowery kimono type dress, out of breath and sweating profusely, walks up to the bench and sits on the false teeth, she starts wiping sweat with a towel as she rests.

G.I. finishes rinsing his mouth and walks back over to the other members of the Senior Gang. The obese woman stands, walks over to the fountain and starts splashing water on her face. G.I. feels his bottom gums and quickly walks back to the bench, his teeth are gone, he starts to search for them by looking all around and under the bench. Speed glances up at the obese woman and notices that the teeth has become lodged in her butt crack, he lets out a laugh then quickly tries to muffle and contain it. Cowboy turns to face Speed with a curious look on his face. "What is it Speed?"

Speed points toward the obese woman. Cowboy sees what Speed was laughing at and starts to try and contain his own laughter, he looks at Speed and they both burst into laughter, then once again try to contain it. "You two are like a couple of kids. What's so funny?" Super Granny asks.

Cowboy bobs his head to motion toward the obese woman. Super Granny sees the false teeth and shakes her head. The rest of the Senior Gang also notice whats going on and all start to giggle. Mr. Fix-it squints, trying to see what's going on. "What is it?"

Lady Po Po whispers in his ear then they both start laughing. The Obese woman dries off with her towel and starts to walk on, as she approaches the Senior Gang, the Gang try to contain their laughter and smile as she passes. Cowboy tries to get G.I.'s attention with out alerting the lady. He starts with a loud whisper. "Hey, G.I., Hey, G.I."

When this gets no results he quickly lets out a loud. "Hey!"

G.I. startled, jumps and turns to face Cowboy. "What?"

Cowboy points at the false teeth as the obese woman walks away. G.I. disappointed and embarrassed, shakes and ducks his head. Wild Rose points toward the obese women. "You better go grab em' G.I. you'll probably need em'."

G.I. shakes his head. "No way, I don't want those no more. I always carry reinforcements anyway."

G.I. reaches in his pocket, pulls out another bottom false teeth plate and places it in his mouth. The rest of the Senior Gang can now hardly contain their laughter. Speed gets a serious look on his face and looks at G.I. "Hey G.I. what did that poor woman ever do to you?"

G.I. looks at speed with a confused expression. "What do you mean Speed?"

Speed still has a serious look on his face. "I was just trying to figure out why you chewed her butt out."

Everyone except G.I. burst into laughter. Dirty Larry tries to control himself long enough to talk. "No wait, he wasn't chewing her out he was just talking to her. You know, Just chewing the fat."

Once again everyone, except G.I. burst into laughter. G.I. shakes his head. "You guys think your funny don't ya?"

Lady Po Po pats G.I. on the back. "Now you all just leave poor G.I. alone it's not his fault."

G.I. Smiles at her. "Thank you Lady Po Po, Wait what's not my fault?"

Lady Po Po shakes her head as though she's showing sympathy. "I seen it every day as a vice cop, with all the other drug addicts. It's not your fault, it's an addiction and you may not have known that crack causes tooth loss."

Everyone bursts into laughter. Dirty Larry is rolling on the ground holding his sides, because he's laughing so hard. G.I. shakes his head once more. "Hardy har har, all of ya are just a bunch of comedians, but that's okay, cause I'm a soldier and this ain't the first time this has happened to me."

Everyone stops laughing and looks at G.I. "Ain't the first time what's happened to you G.I.?" Super Granny asks.

G.I. winks. "As a soldier this ain't the first time I lost a tooth or two in some crappy valley."

Everyone including G.I. burst into laughter.

Pine Ridge nursing home...

At the nurses station Nurse Ogle, looking through her pop-bottle style glasses with really big eyes, punches numbers into a telephone.

Outskirts of Bomar City...

A two-story house, it's the same house Super Granny used as a home for troubled teens, it's a little older, the paint is faded, but it has been maintained. The sign in the front yard has been covered with a tarp, that is tied on with ropes. There is a telephone ringing from inside the house.

Inside...

A good sized foyer, various doors leading to other rooms, stairs leading to the second story, various foyer type furniture and a telephone on the wall, no one is present. The telephone continues to ring. Sherrie Elam, Danny's fiance, a *fancy* looking slightly over weight women, walks into the room and looks around to see if anyone else is coming to answer the telephone. The telephone rings again. "Fine, I'll answer it myself." Sherrie says.

Sherrie stomps over to the telephone and answers it. "Hello?"

Nurse Ogle addresses her from the other end of the line. "Hello, I'm Nurse Ogle with Pine Ridge Nursing Home, may I speak to Danny Hudson, Please?"

"I'm not sure if he's available, I'm his fiance, can you tell me what you need?" Sherrie asks.

"No ma'am, I better tell Mr. Hudson directly,

I'm afraid it's bad news concerning his mother, Grace Hudson." Nurse Ogle says.

Sherrie can't contain her excitement. "Really?"

Sherrie manages to compose herself, before continuing. "Um, I mean, oh my, how awful. Let me see if I can get Danny to come to the phone."

Sherrie sets the telephone down and does a little *victory* dance, then tries to compose herself and tries to sound concerned, as she yells for Danny. "Danny, it's for you."

There is no answer so she tries again. "Danny, phone. It's the nursing home, somethings happened to your mother."

Danny Hudson, Super Granny's adopted son, who is now a heavy set man in his mid thirties, runs through one of the doors, with a fearful look on his face. "What? What happened to mom?"

Sherrie shrugs, as she hands Danny the phone. "I don't know you'll have to ask them."

Sherrie exits the room almost doing the cha-cha with small movements, trying to hide her joy. Danny doesn't notice, his focus is on finding out what is wrong with Super Granny, as he puts the phone to his ear. "Hello?"

"Is this Danny Hudson?" Nurse Ogle asks.

"Yes, it is." Says Danny.

"I'm Nurse Ogle with Pine...."

"I know. What's wrong with my mom?" Danny says.

"There's nothing wrong with her, it's just that, well, she escaped."

"So she's not sick or anything?" Danny asks.

"No sir."

"Thank Goodness, Wait a minute did you say she escaped?"

"Yes sir. Her and a few of the other residents that she congregates with escaped this morning." Nurse Ogle says.

"*Escaped*? What are they prisoners?"

"No sir, what I mean is, well..."

"What you mean is you lost them or let them wonder off and you don't know where they are."

"Well, I suppose you could put it that way." Nurse Ogle says.

"That's exactly how I put it. Did you call the Police?"

"Yes sir, the Police have been notified."

"Good. Do you have my cellphone number?" Danny asks.

Nurse Ogle looks at her computer screen. "Let me see, is it five-five-five-two-zero-one-zero?"

"Yes, that's it. I'm going to go look for them myself, if you hear from them or hear anything about them you call me on that number immediately." Danny says.

"Yes sir, immediately, I will as soon as I hear anything."

"Okay, Thank you." Danny says.

Danny hangs up the telephone and grabs a set of keys off a near by desk. Sherrie comes back into the room. "Where are you going?"

"My mom wondered off from the nursing home, I'm gonna go look for her."

Sherrie gets a disappointed look on her face. "She's not dead?"

Danny is confused by Sherrie's question. "What? What do you mean dead?"

"I mean, well, I just assumed."

Sherrie tries to act happy. "But that's great, she's alive whoopee."

Danny lets it slide, he doesn't have time to deal with it now. "Yea, listen I got to go, just watch Jimmy for me until I get back."

Sherrie gets a shocked look on her face. "What, no, I mean I'm not comfortable with watching him by myself, yet."

"What do you mean not comfortable? He's just a little boy, playing in his room, it won't take much effort. We're getting married in a few weeks and you can't watch my son for a little while?" Danny asks.

"It's just that, I'm not used to kids. It will just take a little time is all." Sherrie says.

Once again Danny doesn't have time to deal with this right now. "Fine, you can go with me and we'll drop Jimmy off at the Morgans."

Danny heads upstairs to get Jimmy, Sherrie

smiles smugly.

Chapter 5
Running Wild With the Beast

A carnival...

The Carnival is located in a large open lot or Field at the edge of Bomar City limits, it has various Attractions (games, rides, events, etc.) scattered about. Lots of people, adults and children move around enjoying the various attractions. The Senior Gang are walking around checking out the attractions, when they get to the wrestling ring, Wild Rose spots a sign that reads: "*Compete against the Beast to win cash money -- Stay in ring for 3 minutes win $500 -- Defeat the Beast and win $1000.*" Wild Rose points to the sign. "Hey guys, look at that."

Super Granny reads the sign, then looks at Wild Rose. "Are you thinking what I think your thinking Rose?"

Wild Rose smiles and nods her head. Super Granny looks to the center of the ring and sees, the

55

Beast, a huge, hairy two hundred and eighty plus pound man of solid muscle in his mid thirties, stomping and growling in the ring like a wild man. Super Granny looks at Wild Rose with a concerned look on her face. "I know we could use the money, but are you sure about this Rose?"

"I'm sure."

Super Granny looks at the Beast and is still worried. "He's awful big and..."

"Super Granny, I can take him." Wild Rose says.

Super Granny may be worried, but she believes in her friend, so she smiles and nods. "Okay."

Wild Rose climbs up to the edge of the ring, as the rest of the Senior Gang sit in the front row seats. Stan, a short heavy set ring announcer in his fifties, is leaning against the ropes, he looks up to see Wild Rose climbing into the ring. Stan quickly runs over to Wild Rose. "Excuse me lady are you lost? Do you need help?"

"I wanna fight the Beast."

Stan is shocked that this frail old lady would even consider such a thing. He thinks she must be senile or just plain crazy. "No. If you got hurt our insurance wouldn't cover it. I can't let a woman as ol, um your ag, um I can't let a women of your maturity and stature compete, I'm sorry. Do you need me to help you out of the ring?"

"What's your name?" Wild Rose asks.

"It's Stan ma'am."

Wild Rose steps up close to Stan and looks him in the eyes. "Well Stan you never mind bout my ma's shirty or my stasher. I've been fightin' men like that since I was knee high to a horn toad and I was born stubborn, so unless ya think you can get me out of this ring, I aim ta fight that feller."

Stan starts to get angry. "Look lady..."

He was raised to respect his elders, so he takes a deep breath and calms himself. "Okay, I'm sorry ma'am, but no offense your a little old lady and he's, well look at him he's a beast. Again no offense, but who do you think you are?"

"Most folks call me Wild Rose."

Stan smiles. "That's nice ma'am, but..."

Stan pauses when he recognizes the name. "Wait did you say Wild Rose?"

"Yes sir."

"The Wild Rose?" Stan asks.

"I reckon, unless ya know someone else called Wild Rose."

"The undefeated Wild Rose from Boon County?" Stan asks.

"That's me, Stan." Wild Rose says with a smile.

Stan grabs Wild Rose's hand with both of his and starts shaking it. He can't contain his excitement. "Why didn't you say so in the first place? I'm your biggest fan, I was there back in '68' when you threw that big hillbilly out of the ring, it would be an honor to see you fight again."

Stan continues to shake Wild Rose's hand. "Stan?" Wild Rose says.

Stan is still excited. "Yes ma'am?"

Wild Rose smiles. "It's a pleasure ta meet you too, but do ya reckon I could get my hand back?"

"Stan realizes what he's doing and smiles as his face turns a light shade of red, he gives Wild Rose's hand a little pat and releases it. "Sorry ma'am, I'm just so excited."

"That's okay, how about we get started?" Wild Rose asks.

Stan winks. "Yes ma'am."

Stan walks over to pick up his microphone at the edge of the ring.

In the front row...

The Senior Gang are watching on, waiting for the match to start. "He sure is an excited little fella ain't he?" Speed says.

Cowboy nods. "Ya got that right Speed."

"You two hush up." Super Granny says.

Super Granny turns her attention back to the ring and yells encouragement to Wild Rose. "Come on wild rose you can do it."

Mr. Fix-it turns and looks at Lady Po Po and yells. "Come on Wild Rose give him a whipping."

Lady Po Po leans away and covers her ear, Super Granny grabs Mr. Fix-it's head and gently turns it to face the ring. All the remaining Senior Gang start to cheer Wild Rose on.

In the ring...

The Beast is hitting one palm with his other fist, with a grimace on his face. Wild Rose is using the ropes to stretch and warm up. Stan paces at the front of the ring addressing the audience. "Ladies and gentlemen we have a special guest today. Wild Rose is here to tame the Beast. When you hear the bell all chaos will break loose."

Stan steps out of the ring and grabs the small hammer hanging from the bell on the corner of the ring. The Beast steps to the center of the ring. Wild Rose turns and faces him, Stan rings the bell. The Beast sees Wild Rose and gets a confused look on his face. "Wait a second, no way, stop the fight."

"Come on Beast whats the hold up? People want to see a fight." Stan says.

The Beast shakes his head. "I ain't fighting no old lady. What are you trying to pull Stan?"

"She's a professional, you might be surprised by what she can do, she won't hurt you to bad, maybe. Now fight." Stan says

The Beast folds his arms across his chest and shakes his head. "No, I ain't fighting no old lady, you can forget it."

Wild Rose walks up to the Beast and flips him on the nose with her finger. The Beast grabs his nose in pain and steps back. "Ow, stop it lady."

Wild Rose motions with her hands to come on. "Come on you sissy lets fight."

The Beast shakes his head, no. Wild Rose walks up to him and pokes him in the eye. The Beast grabs his eye in pain. "Ow, quit it lady, I ain't fighting you."

Wild Rose approaches the Beast again. The Beast quickly covers his face with his hands. Wild Rose kicks him in the shin. The Beast grabs his shin and hops around while rubbing it. "Ow, ow, ow, stop doing stuff to me, there's nothing you can do to make me fight you."

Wild Rose knows she needs to do something drastic to get the Beast to fight. Not only does the Senior Gang need the money, but Wild Rose needs to cut loose. She's been bottled up to long and needs to let the wild run free. Wild Rose grabs the Beast's nipples and twists hard. The Beast steps back and slaps Wild Rose's hands away and gives her an angry look, as he rubs his nipples. "No one gives me a purple nurple, no one. You've gone to far now, you wanted a fight, well now you got one lady."

That must have been the right buttons to twist so to speak, the Beast puts up his fist in a fighting pose. Wild Rose smiles and squares off against him.

In front row...

Cowboy has a confused look on his face and taps Super Granny on the shoulder. "What did he just call that?"

Super Granny turns to answer. "A purple nurple."

Cowboy gets a more confused look on his face. "Why?"

Super Granny pauses for a moment to figure out how to best explain it. She decides the best way is to just say it straight. "Well, nurple is a reference to a nipple and when someone pinches and twists like that, well it turns your nurples purple, so they call it a purple nurple."

Cowboy shakes his head. "That's not what they call it in Texas."

Super Granny smiles and shakes her head as she turns back toward the ring.

In the ring...

The Beast is growling and snarling at Wild Rose as both opponents circle around the ring. The Beast rushes toward Wild Rose and tries to take her down. Wild Rose quickly puts her foot up, rolls to her back and throws the Beast over her head using a Judo move called a *Tomoe-nage*. The Beast's momentum carries him forward and he lands hard on his back with a grunt. Both opponents quickly stand to face each other again.

61

The Beast punches Wild Rose in the face, then turns, and wraps his arm around Wild Rose's neck to put her in a headlock with both of them facing the same direction. The Beast continues to punch Wild Rose in the face.

In front row...

The rest of the Senior Gang all cringe as Wild Rose is being hit in the face. Super Granny covers her eyes. "I can't watch, maybe we should stop the fight."

Speed shakes his head. "If we stopped this fight Wild Rose would have our hides. Besides she's a tough lady and I think she's fixin' ta turn things around."

In the ring...

Wild Rose grabs the arm that the Beast is punching her with and holds it so he can't punch her again. Wild Rose reaches the arm closest to the Beast, behind him and smashes it into his groin. The Beast makes a painful face and stoops just a bit in a weakened state. Wild Rose grabs his leg and does a forward roll, rolling both herself and the Beast, they wind up on their backs and Wild Rose has the Beast in a leg lock. Wild Rose pulls back on the Beast's leg. The Beast grits his teeth in pain, as Wild Rose smashes her elbow into his face. The Beast is knocked senseless and is in an obvious daze.

Wild Rose quickly jumps up, gets behind the Beast, raises him to a seated position and wraps her arms around his neck in a sleeper hold. Within seconds you can see the Beast batting his eyes and trying to remain conscious. The Beast rapidly taps Wild Rose's leg three times as he gives, the fight is over. Wild Rose lets go and steps back. The Beast slumps to the mat as he gasps for air, then looks up at Wild Rose and smiles. "Your good lady, the best I've ever fought."

Wild Rose smiles back. "Thank ya. Yore pretty good yore self young man."

Wild Rose extends her hand and helps the Beast up off the mat and gives him a hug and a pat on the back. You can hear the rest of the Senior Gang whooping, hollering and cheering. Stan steps back into the ring and holds Wild Rose's arm over her head as he addresses the crowd. "Ladies and gentlemen we have a winner. Still undefeated, Wild Rose takes another victory."

Stan hands Wild Rose ten crisp one-hundred dollar bills. "You earned this thousand dollars, Wild Rose ma'am. It's the best thousand dollars I've ever spent. Most heroes fall from grace, I'm glad to see mine is still the best."

Wild Rose humbly smiles and gives Stan a hug, before climbing out of the ring to rejoin her friends.

Chapter 6
Guns for a Cowboy

Later...

In front of the tilt-o-whirl, the Senior Gang are counting the money that Wild Rose Just won. When they finish Wild Rose puts the money away. The Senior Gang look across the pathway and see a big Strongman in a leopard skin outfit, motioning for them. The Senior Gang walk over and the strong man picks up a thick still bar and bends it into a *U*, then hands it to Speed. "I think he wants you to try and bend it Speed, he must not be able to talk." Super Granny says.

The Strongman nods, Speed grits and groans as he tries to bend the bar, but it doesn't budge. The Strongman smiles and points to G.I., G.I. grabs the bar and gives it a try. The bar doesn't budge. G.I. puts his cigar in his mouth and tries again. The bar

65

moves a little, but not much, G.I. shakes his head and smiles. The Strongman points to Dirty Larry, Dirty Larry smiles, grabs the bar and hands it to Wild Rose.

The Strongman smiles and motions for her to try it. Wild Rose bends the bar until the two ends touch, then bends it back out into a *U* shape, then hands it back to the Strongman. The Strongman's mouth falls open in shock, he grabs the bar and squeezes, but can't get it past the *U* shape. Dirty Larry pats the Strongman on the back. "You just keep working out and you'll get it one day."

The Strongman smiles and bows, conceding to Wild Rose. The Senior Gang move on, Speed looks in the near distance and gets a love struck look in his eyes and stops, mesmerized he stares unblinkingly. Dirty Larry notices speed. "Hey guys whats wrong with speed?"

Everyone looks at Speed. Cowboy walks over and looks at his face and waves his hand in front of his eyes. Speed continues to stare in the same direction with a blank look. Cowboy stares close at Speeds eyes as though he's trying to look inside his head. "Ya okay Speed? Speed? Speed? You in there buddy? What is it?"

Speed unable to speak, slowly raises his arm and points in the direction he is looking. The Senior Gang all look to see what Speed is looking at.

The shooting gallery...

The shooting gallery has a wild west theme about it and has a short range for revolvers and a longer range for rifles, each have round metal targets at the end. Behind the booth is William, an average built man with long hair, a handle bar mustache and chin puff and wearing a fringed buckskin jacket and cowboy hat. He looks or is trying to look like William F. "Buffalo Bill" Cody.

Beside the gallery is three rotating prize pedestals. On the first pedestal is a motorcycle. On the second pedestal is a four door luxury car. On the third pedestal is a beautiful, customized passenger van, it's big enough to accommodate all of the Senior Gang and a couple more, it is also what has Speed's attention.

There is a large banner in front of the pedestals with three lines of phrases on it. The first line reads: "*$25 gets you a chance to shoot 6 targets with a revolver to win a custom motorcycle.*" The second line reads: "*$50 gets you a chance to shoot 12 targets with a rifle to win a custom car.*" The third line reads: "*$100 gets you a chance to shoot both 6 targets with a revolver and 12 targets with a rifle to win a custom van.*"

A short distance away...
Super Granny realizing what Speed sees, smiles

and nods. "It's the van at the shooting gallery."

Lady Po Po sees the van, smiles and nods. "Yea I see it. You like that van Speed?"

Speed still in a love struck daze smiles and nods slowly. Cowboy points to the banner. "That banner says we can win it, lets give it a try."

"I don't know. Do you see the price to try?" Super Granny asks.

Cowboy tilts his hat back just a little. "Yea, but if we win, it'd be worth it."

Super Granny is still skeptical and trying to reason this out with logic. "There's no guarantee we will win though and if we all try that will be eight hundred dollars."

Cowboy pushes his hat back a little higher and smiles. "Come on we can do it."

"I'd like to try." Lady Po Po says.

"Me too." Dirty Larry says.

"Yea I bet one of us could do it." Mr. Fix-it says as he stares at a near by post thinking it's Super Granny.

Wild Rose gives Super Granny a little bump with her elbow. "What do ya say Super Granny?"

Super Granny looks at G.I. for his opinion. "You got any words of advice G.I."

G.I. pulls a cigar out of his pocket and puts it in his mouth. "A British friend of mine used to say, Those who dares, wins".

Super Granny is considered the brains of this

operation, so she usually has the final say, she's still pondering the idea as she addresses Speed. "Speed you think you can drive that if we do manage to win it?"

Speed snaps out of his daze and looks at Super Granny with a look on his face that makes her realize she just asked a stupid question. "Sorry, that's like asking a fish if he can swim. Okay, lets give it a try."

Everyone excitedly rushes toward the shooting gallery.

The shooting gallery...

William smugly smiles as he sees the Senior Gang approaching. "Step right up folks, this here is easy winnings. Pick yore challenge twenty-five, fifty or the one-hundred dollar challenge the choice is yours."

As the Senior Gang reach the booth they all huddle together. "Okay, who's going first." Super Granny asks.

Cowboy is the first to speak up, or at least tries to. "I think..."

"I want to go first, I'm so excited and I think I can use that." Speed says.

Cowboy tries again. "Alright, that's fine then after him I..."

Super Granny holds her hand up to stop Cowboy before he finishes. "Sorry to interrupt

Cowboy, but I think Speed should go first since he was the first to notice it. Then G.I. cause he has military experience, then Lady Po Po cause she has law enforcement training. Then Dirty Larry, Wild Rose, Mr. Fix-it, me and then you Cowboy."

Cowboy tries again to speak his mind. "But I..."

"Yea I agree that sounds the most logical." Lady Po Po says.

"So does everyone else agree?" Super Granny asks.

G.I. takes the cigar out of his mouth and puts it back in his pocket. "Yes ma'am."

"Agreed." Dirty Larry says.

"Works for me." Mr. Fix-it says talking to a flagpole.

"That's fine an dandy with me." Wild Rose says.

Cowboy is disappointed, but goes along anyway. "Yes ma'am I reckon we can go in that order."

Speed steps up to the booth and sees an *Uberti 1885 Army Outlaw* revolver and a *Winchester 30-30* lever-action rifle, laying on the booth. William is feeling pretty good about his prospects. "What challenge ya want ta try old timer?"

Speed points to the van. "We're all gonna try to win the van."

Wild Rose lays a hundred dollar bill down on the booth. William picks up the money and holds it up to the sun to check if its real, then smiles and puts it in a box behind the booth. "My names William and I'll be glad to take all yore money. It works like this old timer ya shoot six targets in the short range with the revolver, then ya shoot twelve targets in the long range with the rifle, if ya hit every target ya win the van, however if ya miss even one it's game over and ya gotta stop shootin', no point in wastin' ammo after ya done lost. Go ahead and giver a try."

Speed picks up the revolver, cocks the hammer, aims and fires, hitting one of the steel targets and knocking it over. Speed cocks the hammer again, aims, fires and hits another target. The Senior Gang get excited, but try to contain it, as to not make Speed nervous. Speed once more cocks the hammer, aims, fires and misses, disappointed he hands the revolver to William and turns to face the Senior Gang. William grins. "Better luck next time old timer. Who's next?"

G.I. pats Speed on the back as he passes. "That's okay Speed you did good."

Speed nods. "Thanks G.I., it seems ta shoot a little to the left so ya might wanna try an compensate for it."

G.I. nods back and steps up to the booth. The rest of the Senior Gang pat Speed on the back and console him. Wild Rose gives William another one-hundred dollar bill. William hands the reloaded revolver to G.I. and looks him over. "I can tell by the way you look and carry yourself yore a military man, maybe you'll do a little better, not likely, but we can hope."

G.I. pulls a cigar out of his pocket and puts it in his mouth and gives William a tough as nails look. William ducks his head and shuts his mouth. G.I. picks up the revolver, cocks the hammer, aims and fires, knocking one of the reset targets down. He fires another shot and it hits it's mark. The third shot also hits a target.

The Senior Gang again get excited. G.I. fires a fourth shot and it knocks another target over. The fifth shot knocks a target over as G.I. smiles. He fires the sixth shot and misses, disappointed he hands the revolver to William and waits for a remark. William takes the revolver and says nothing as he avoids eye contact.

Lady Po Po steps up to take her turn, she picks up the revolver aims down range, fires and hits one of the reset targets. She fires another shot and misses, she lowers the revolver with a disappointed look on her face. The Senior Gang console her as she steps away from the booth. William again gets that smug grin on his face. "Send the next one up, I got bills ta pay."

Dirty Larry steps up, as Wild Rose lays another one-hundred dollar bill on the table. William sees Dirty Larry's appearance, grabs the money and steps back a few feet. Dirty Larry picks up the revolver and aims down range, he has his tongue stuck out and his body leaning forward really focused and braced. He lowers the revolver slightly and looks down range then raises and re-aims. Dirty Larry wipes his eyes with one hand then re-grabs and re-aims, again really focused. William is shaking his head and getting frustrated and impatient. Dirty Larry finally fires and misses, he examines the revolver like there is definitely something wrong with it. William grabs a rag and wipes off the revolver, before reloading it. "who's next?"

Wild Rose lays another one-hundred dollar bill on the table. "It's ma turn?"

"This may be to much gun for a' little missy like you." William says.

Before Wild Rose can respond, the Beast grabs William from behind and turns him around to face him. "That little *missy* just won that money by whipping my butt. So I suggest you show her some respect. If ya don't she may show ya her true size and I'll finish off whats left."

William swallows hard and doesn't say a word. The Beast puts his hand gently on Wild Rose's shoulder. "It was an honor to meet you ma'am, good luck."

Wild Rose smiles. "Same here and thank ya."

The Beast points his finger at William and walks away. Wild Rose aims the revolver down

73

range, fires and misses. She hands the revolver back to William with both anger and disappointment. William hesitantly takes the revolver and ducks his head. Wild Rose puts another hundred dollar bill on the table and steps to the side.

Mr. Fix-it walks up and stops after he bumps into the table. He leans in close to the table and grabs the revolver. He squints and raises the revolver up to his face really close trying to see. He starts to pan the revolver around and points it at William. William quickly pushes the revolver away and points it down range. "Hey! Watch where you point that, ya gotta keep it pointed down range."

Mr. Fix-it, still squinting, again starts to pan the revolver toward William. William grabs the barrel and pushes it away until it points down range and this time he holds it in place. "Okay fella I think you best just pull the trigger right there."

Mr. Fix-it pulls the trigger and fires. We can see the bullet hit the ground about halfway down the range. William takes the revolver out of Mr. Fix-it's hands. Mr. Fix-it leans forward and squints real hard. "Did I get It? I think I hit something."

William grins. "Ya didn't hit it, but ya got real close."

It's now Super Granny's turn, she aims the revolver down range, fires and hits one of the targets. She cocks the hammer again and fires, but misses the target, she shakes her head in disappointment, as she hands the revolver to William. William reloads the revolver. "Who's next?"

Super Granny shakes her head. "I think we spent enough money, we better call it quits while we still have some left."

Cowboy steps forward. "Wait, I haven't had my turn yet."

William chuckles and shakes his head as he looks Cowboy over. "Yea ya are ta' give the little feller a turn."

Cowboy ignores him and continues to plead with Super Granny. "Just one chance is all I ask, if I miss I'll find a' way ta pay back the whole thousand."

Super Granny feels sorry for him, but wishes she would have stopped this a long time ago. "I don't know Cowboy we all tried and didn't even come close."

Cowboy takes his hat off. "Yea, but I didn't even get to try."

Wild Rose holds up a one-hundred dollar bill ready to put it on the table. "He's right Super Granny, every one else went."

Lady Po Po nods in agreement. "It's only fair that he gets a turn too."

G.I. pulls the cigar out of his mouth and puts it

in his pocket. "We're a team each of us should have the right to try what everyone else does. We don't leave a man behind."

Super Granny is ashamed she even considered it and shakes her head. "Okay, okay, your right. Have you ever fired a gun before Cowboy?"

Cowboy puts his hat back on and smiles. "Yes ma'am, a couple a' times."

Granny nods and smiles, but you can tell she's not very confident. "Do your your best."

Wild Rose puts the one-hundred dollar bill on the table, as Cowboy steps up to the booth. William hands him the revolver with a smug smile. "Ya need me ta help ya cock the hammer back little fella?"

Cowboy pulls his hat down a little in front. "No, I believe I can manage it on my own."

William lets out a little chuckle. "Feeling a little spunky today uh?"

Cowboy ignores him and holds the revolver sideways in one extended hand, closes one eye and looks down the barrel to examine it, the barrel is bent. Cowboy lowers the revolver and looks at William, who still has a smug smile on his face. "Yea, I see what kind of con game your running now."

William's smile turns to an angry look. "Ya best watch yore accusations old man. Now shoot or walk away."

Cowboy smiles and looks back down range, he smoothly spins the revolver backward around his finger several times, then catches it and rapidly fans the hammer and fires six shots. Every shot hits a target and all six targets fall. Everyone opens there mouth in surprise. Cowboy lays the revolver down on the booth and picks up the rifle, turns to look at the rest of the Senior Gang and winks. Cowboy looks down the rifle range and rapidly levers and fires twelve shots, every shot hits and knocks over a target. Cowboy spins the rifle, like the Rifleman® and throws it on the booth and looks at William. "I reckon I was feeling a little spunky."

William gets an angry look on his face. "Y'all need ta leave right now."

Cowboy puts his hands on the booth and leans toward William. "Listen here little Bill. You just cheated my friends out a' seven hundred dollars, but we'll over look it if you honor the challenge that I just Won. So ya need ta do any paper work ya need and give us the keys ta that there van and ya best treat me and my friends with respect from here on out, other wise the next thing I knock over ain't gonna be a' steel target. Ya understand me Bill?"

William's anger turns to fear, he pulls a slip of paper out from under the table and hands it to Cowboy. "Yes sir, you can take this up to the office, it's the trailer at the south entrance."

William's demeanor has changed and he is now speaking with respect. "I'll go get everything ready and you can pick up the van when ya leave."

Cowboy holds up the slip of paper. "This good?"

William nods. "Yes sir, it's good they'll know what it is at the office."

Cowboy squints, he is now looking less like an accountant and more like an old west gunfighter. "It better be and ya best get those barrels straightened."

William nods and walks away. The Senior Gang excitedly pat Cowboy on the back and show him their proud of him. Super Granny ducks her head, then looks back up at Cowboy. "I guess we all owe you an apology, don't we? Me most of all."

Cowboy shakes his head. "No ma'am that won't be necessary."

Super Granny smiles. "Well, from now on when we call you Cowboy it will have a different ring to it and it will definitely be said with more respect."

"Thanks Super Granny." Cowboy says.

Super Granny squints one eye and tilts her head to the side. "Now just one more thing, I thought you were an accountant?"

Cowboy nods. "I was during the week, but on the weekends I did what I loved, I performed in a wild west show."

Cowboy looks up and to the side as though he is remembering something, as he tells his full story.

1972 – Wild West Show...

A large arena with spectator seating all around it, there is a large banner that reads: "*Hillbilly Coon Dog's extremely exciting, positively alluring, wild west extravaganza.*"

In a booth overlooking the arena, Hillbilly Coon Dog, A large man in his late fifties, wearing overalls and a coon skin hat, with a full, grayed beard, places a megaphone to his mouth. "Now lady's and gentlemen, the one you all been waiting for, he's an expert rider and an expert marksman, lets hear it for the man simply known as Cowboy."

In the arena...

There are twelve balloons lined up in a row in the middle of the arena. A young Cecil "Cowboy" Poindexter, a slim, young man in his late twenties wearing a *cowboy outfit*, comes riding into the arena on a graceful chestnut mare. He stands up in the saddle, places the reins in his mouth and draws two revolvers from the holster he's wearing. He rapidly alternates firing each revolver until he has burst all twelve balloons, then he drops back to a seated position in the saddle.

Cowboy grabs a lever-action rifle from the scabbard, hangs off one side with his leg hooked on the saddle horn and rapidly levers and fires the rifle several times, each shot hits a steel target, located at the other end of the arena. Cowboy sits back up in the saddle, places the rifle back in the scabbard, then drops off one side of the saddle and bounces up to the other side then back to the saddle. Cowboy brings his horse to a sliding stop, rolls of the back and lands on his feet, he stands next to his horse, takes his hat off and takes a bow. He raises back up and points to his horse with his hat, who also takes a bow. Cowboy raises his hat above his head and the crowd goes wild with cheers and excitement.

Present day...

All the Senior Gang are still at the shooting gallery booth listening intently to Cowboy's story."And that was my passion, accounting was so boring , but the wild west shows kept me happy."

Super Granny smiles when Cowboy finishes his story and gives him a hug. "So that's what you meant when you talked about your horse."

Cowboy nods. "Yes ma'am. I knew you all thought I was a crazy old man."

Dirty Larry shakes his head. "Not me, it never crossed my mind, I believed you from the very beginning."

The Senior Gang cannot keep from laughing about Dirty Larry's lies. Dirty Larry rubs his belly.

"I'm hungry, how about we go get a hotdog?"

"I could go for good dawg myself." Speed says.

Wild Rose holds up what money she has left. "I'm buying."

G.I. gently nudges Wild Rose with his elbow. "Good, cause your the only one with any money."

The Senior Gang head off, all in good spirits.

Chapter 7
Vision Quest

Later at the porta-john area...

In this area there is a row of Porta-Johns against a fence and in front of these there is a row of benches facing the Porta-Johns. Lady Po Po, Super Granny, Mr. Fix-it, Wild Rose and Cowboy are all sitting on the benches bent-over holding their stomachs, sick from the hot dogs. Dirty Larry and G.I. are just fine standing near the benches watching on. Speed comes stumbling out of one of the Porta-Johns holding his stomach with one hand and his nose with the other. "Ugh, I don't know what smells worse, what was already in there or what just come out a' me."

Speed sits down on one of the benches next to the rest of the gang. Super Granny manages to compose herself enough to address G.I. and Dirty Larry. "How come you two didn't get sick?"

G.I. puts his cigar back in his mouth. "In the

83

Army we had to be able to be dropped behind enemy lines and survive for however long it took, on whatever was available, so we were trained to eat things that would make a billy goat puke."

Everyone looks at Dirty Larry to hear his response. Dirty Larry shrugs his shoulders "I've ate billy goat puke."

The entire Senior Gang except G.I. and Dirty Larry hold their stomach's with one hand and cover their mouth's with the other and rush into the Porta-Johns.

Dirty Larry looks at G.I. and shrugs again. "I guess they didn't like my answer."

G.I. puts the cigar back in his pocket. "What gave you that idea?"

Dirty Larry and G.I. have a good chuckle. Dirty Larry points to the benches. "Is it just me or is it strange that the benches face the toilets? Does people actually sit out here and watch others go to the bathroom?"

"You'd be surprised at what people do anymore besides with the food they serve here they might get a pretty good show." G.I. says.

Dirty Larry smiles. "We just did."

Dirty Larry and G.I. have another good chuckle then sit on the benches to wait for the rest of the gang.

Later...

The Senior Gang's van is now traveling on a four-lane street, in Bomar City. The interior of the van has two bucket seats in front with a center console, behind this is three rows of bench seats. The van could seat eleven people comfortably. Speed is driving, G.I. is in the front passenger seat. In the bench seat behind them is Super Granny on the passenger side and Dirty Larry on the drivers side. In the middle bench seat is Mr. Fix-it on the drivers side and Lady Po Po on the passengers side. In the rear bench seat is Cowboy on the drivers side and Wild Rose on the passengers side. "Where to now, guys?" Speed asks.

"I guess we should have decided that before we left, but we was all to excited to try the van out." Super Granny says.

A bug splatters on the windshield and Dirty Larry reaches up and punches Speed in the arm as hard as he can."A dead one."

The van swerves into the oncoming traffic lane and narrowly avoids two cars as they honk, then Speed jerks the wheel trying to get the van back to the original lane. Speed struggles and gets the van back under control and rubs his arm. "What was that for?"

Dirty Larry points to the splattered bug. "It's a game called Slug Bug, every time you see a bug you slug someone in the arm and then describe the bug."

85

Speed shakes his head. "Would someone explain that game to him, before he gets us all killed?"

Super Granny Whispers in Dirty Larry's ear to explain it to him. Dirty Larry makes a face like he just learned something really good. "That makes a lot of sense, now I know how to play it."

A yellow Volkswagen Beetle car passes them going the opposite way. Speed tenses up and prepares for a punch. Dirty Larry smiles and makes a fist, but before he can do anything, Super Granny slugs him in the arm as hard as she can. "Yellow one."

Dirty Larry grabs his arm and falls back in his seat. "Ow!"

Dirty Larry looks confused as he rubs his arm. The rest of the Senior Gang smile. "That games not any fun lets not play it anymore."

Later...

The van, still traveling on a four-lane street, is in the left hand lane as it pulls up to an intersection and stops at a red light. There is a gas station on the far side corner, with a sign that reads: "*Get food and fuel here.*" Dirty Larry points at the gas station sign. "Hey, that sign says we can eat and get gas there."

Super Granny looks at Dirty Larry with a surprised look. "You can't possibly be hungry already, you ate ten hot dogs at the carnival."

Speed looks at the fuel gauge. "The van's full we don't need any gas."

Dirty Larry raises up and farts then smiles proudly. Mr. Fix-it is the first to smell it, he turns his head and makes a sour face as he grabs his nose. "Dirty Larry is full of gas too."

Super Granny flings the side door open and sticks her head out. Mr. Fix-it sticks his head out the side door with Super Granny, gasping for fresh air. Lady Po Po leans over trying to get some air too. G.I. and Speed both roll their windows down and stick their heads out. Cowboy and Wild Rose both cover their faces with their shirt tails and hands. "Oh my gawd, that smells worse than a pole cat and we ain't got no winders back here." Wild Rose says.

Another car pulls up on the passenger side of the van and stops at the red light. The Driver, a fancy looking women, is giving the Senior Gang strange looks. There is an Afghan Hound in the back seat of the car with his head stuck out the window.

Mr. Fix-it's point of view...

Mr. Fix-it looks up and sees a scrawny, long nosed young man with long blond hair. "How are you young fella, did someone fart in your car too?"

Actual point of view...

The red light changes to green and the car pulls away. Mr. Fix-it watches the car drive away with an angry look on his face. "Don't you people have any manners?"

Mr. Fix-it looks at Super Granny. "Did you see that little hippie just plain ignore me?"

Super Granny is confused by his statement. "What hipp..."

Then she realizes what he meant and it hits her what Mr. Fix-it's problem has been all along. She's surprised she didn't figure it out sooner, all the signs were there. "Oh! You know people just don't have any manners anymore Mr. Fix-it."

Super Granny pats Mr. Fix-it on the arm as she looks concerned. Mr. Fix-it nods in agreement. Super Granny looks up and smiles as though she just got a great idea. "Speed I know exactly where we need to go next."

Optometrist office...

The Optometrist office is a small, stand alone, brick building, with a sign out front that reads: "*Dr. Ira Seymour, O.D.*"

Inside...

A typical Optometrist exam room with eye charts and equipment. Mr. Fix-it is sitting on the exam table. Dr. Ira Seymour, a small built middle aged eye doctor, is standing next to the exam table holding a occluder, the small hand-held paddle used to cover an eye. "Now Mr. Spencer I'm going to cover each of your eyes, one at a time with this paddle and I want you to read the lowest line you can from the chart on that wall over there, so that we can determine the condition of your vision."

Mr. Fix-it squints and leans forward trying to see the chart. "What chart?"

Dr. Seymour points to the chart on the wall. "That one on the wall there."

Mr. Fix-it squints harder. "I don't see any chart Doc. Wait a minute did the others put you up to this?"

"No Mr. Spencer I'm not joking."

Dr. Seymour walks over to the chart and puts his hand on it. "This chart, Mr. Spencer, are you saying you cannot see this chart at all?"

Mr. Fix-it again squints and leans forward trying to see. "Forget the chart Doc, I can't even see you."

Dr. Seymour nods. "Alright, lets do this another way."

Dr. Seymour pulls a stool up to the exam table then reaches over and pulls a Phoropter in front of Mr. Fix-it's eyes. "Okay Mr. Spencer you look through here and tell me when or if you start to see something."

Mr. Fix-it nods and looks through the

contraption. "Will do Doc."

Later...

Mr. Fix-it walks into the reception area where the rest of the Senior Gang are waiting. The Receptionist, a Gothic looking women with dark make-up and face piercings in her early twenties, is behind the reception counter, chewing gum with an open mouth and a bored, blank look on her face. Lady Po Po is the first to look up and see Mr. Fix-it. "What did the Doctor say Mr. Fix-it?"

Mr. Fix-it holds up a slip of paper. "He gave me a prescription."

"Where do you got to go to get them made?" Lady Po Po asks.

Mr. Fix-it shrugs his shoulders. Dirty Larry gets an idea and gets excited. "How about one of them one-hour photo places?"

Cowboy hits Dirty Larry with his cowboy hat. "Those are for getting pictures developed."

Dirty Larry ducks his head in disappointment. "Well they both have something to do with eyes or seeing or something."

"Wait your close Dirty Larry, there are places that make prescription glasses in an hour." Super Granny says.

"Does anyone know where one of them places is?" Speed asks.

Everyone shrugs their shoulders or shakes their

head. Lady Po Po walks toward the reception desk. "I'm gonna go ask the Receptionist."

Everyone looks at the Receptionist, who still has the same blank, bored look and is chewing her gum with an open mouth. Wild Rose Smiles. "If ya can get her ta stop chewing her cud, ya might get an answer."

Everyone chuckles as Lady Po Po approaches the Receptionist. We cannot hear the conversation but we can see the Receptionist's actions. The Receptionist nods very unenthusiastically several times and then very lazily points to her right. Lady Po Po turns and with a smile walks back to the rest of the Senior Gang. "She said there's one right next door."

Super Granny stands up. "Great lets go."

The Senior Gang all head for the door and exit.

One hour glasses store...

A small room with a desk and chairs, a sign on the desk reads: "*We make things less blurry in a hurry.*" another sign next to that one reads: "*Prescription glasses filled in an hour or less guaranteed.*" The Optician, a very skinny and feminine acting and sounding man with long hair in his early thirties, is rummaging through the desk drawers. There is a row of chairs lined up next to the front entrance. A door to another room has a sign on it that reads: "*Optician only, no one else*

91

beyond this point."

The Senior Gang walk in through the front entrance. The Optician stops what he is doing and approaches them. "Can I help you?"

Mr. Fix-it starts to act shy and nervous. Super Granny lightly nudges him with her elbow. Mr. Fix-it, still acting strange looks around trying to avoid eye contact with the Optician. Super Granny confused, grabs the prescription and hands it to the Optician. "Can you fill this prescription, Sir?"

The Optician takes the prescription and looks it over, then walks to the desk and gets a clipboard with forms in it. He walks back over and hands the clipboard to Super Granny. Super Granny takes the clipboard and waits for the Optician to respond. "Yes ma'am. I can have them ready in an hour you can either wait here or come back later. I need you to fill out that paper work in any case. I'm also running a special today only, you can get it for fifty dollars."

Super Granny nods and smiles. "That will be fine, we'll come back when your finished."

The Optician smiles and nods, then walks through the *Optician only* door. Mr. Fix-it only relaxes when the Optician is out of the room. Super Granny looks at him with a confused stare. "What is wrong with you?"

Mr. Fix-it ducks his head in embarrassment. "Nothing, that glasses lady is kinda pretty ain't she?"

Super Granny looks confused, then realizes what he means and becomes both surprised and amused. "Mr. Fix-it I think you better keep those comments to yourself until you get your glasses."

Mr. Fix-it is confused, but nods in agreement anyway. Super Granny sits in one of the chairs and starts filling out the forms. "I'm gonna fill out these forms, you guys decide where we,re gonna go for an hour."

Dirty Larry looks out the front window. "Hey! There's a museum across the street. We could take in some culture and broaden our minds."

"I don't know about all that, but the museum sounds alright ta me." Speed says.

The rest of the Senior Gang agree by nodding their heads.

Chapter 8
Don't Mess With Seniors

Museum...

The Senior Gang stand in the lobby of a large museum, staring up in awe at a huge tyrannosaurus skeleton in front of them. "I bet he could eat more than me." Dirty Larry says.

Cowboy tilts his hat up just a bit. "I reckon he could eat all of us."

Dirty Larry puts his hand on his belly. "All this talk about eating is making me hungry."

"Everything makes you hungry, Dirty Larry." G.I. says.

Dirty Larry looks at G.I. "I can't help it, I got a fast metabo...metab...metabism..."

"Metabolism." Lady Po Po says.

Dirty Larry points at Lady Po Po. "Yea what she said."

"Okay guys we got one hour so lets all have fun, but make sure your back here in an hour."

95

Super Granny says.

The senior Gang explore the exhibits and all have fun. G.I. goes to a military exhibit and sees a M2 155mm "Long Tom" Towed Gun. He puts a cigar in his mouth and smiles proudly, as he leans against it like it's an old friend.

Mr. Fix-it is squinting, trying to see a painting, he backs into a statue with it's hand out in handshake position, he turns and shakes it's hand, then realizes its a statue. He looks around hoping no one is there and smiles as he realizes he wouldn't know it if they were.

Speed Finds a Prohibition exhibit and runs his hand along a 1940 Ford coupe "bootleggers car." as he admires the detail and remembers the good old times.

Cowboy heads straight to a Wild west exhibit. He sees a display of wax gunfighters, He looks around to make sure no one is watching, then squares off against the wax gunfighters. He pretends to draw, then pretends to blow smoke from his gun barrel and re-holsters. He smiles as he daydreams about what it would be like to live in the wild west.

Super Granny, Lady Po Po, Dirty Larry and Wild Rose visit a Prehistoric exhibit. Dirty Larry pretends to be a caveman and jumps around making silly faces. Super Granny, Lady Po Po and Wild Rose are laughing so hard they have tears running down their faces.

Later...

The Senior Gang all look tired and worn out as they meet back at the lobby. Dirty Larry wipes sweat off of his face. "I didn't know having fun was so much work."

"You think we got time for a nap?" Mr. Fix-it asks.

Super Granny shakes her head. "No, your glasses should be ready by now lets go see."

One hour glasses store...

The Senior Gang walk into the store with Mr. Fix-it in front. The Optician sees them and grabs a pair of glasses and approaches them. Mr. Fix-it stares at him with a funny nervous grin. The Optician hands the glasses to Mr. Fix-it. "I have your glasses ready, try them on."

Mr. Fix-it shyly looks down at the floor and slides one foot around. Super Granny nudges Mr. Fix-it forwards. Still acting shy Mr. Fix-it takes the glasses and raises them to his face, but looks over them at the Optician.

Mr. Fix-it's point of view...

Mr. Fix-it sees a beautiful young woman flirtatiously running her hand through her hair and making kissing gestures at him. Mr. Fix-it puts the glasses on and sees reality.

Actual point of view...

The Optician is scratching his head and making a pucker face. Mr. Fix-it screams and turns to see the Senior Gang and makes another startled expression. "What is it Mr. Fix-it?" Super Granny asks.

Mr. Fix-it points with his thumb over his shoulder. "I thought he was a she, which was a completely innocent mistake that we will never speak of again."

Mr. Fix-it looks over all of the Senior Gang. "And you guys look older than I thought you were."

Everyone looks at Mr. Fix-it with an angry look. "Thanks a lot." Super Granny says.

No, I'm sorry I didn't mean it like that it's just everything looks different and it's gonna take some getting use to." Mr. Fix-it says.

"I think it's safe to say those aren't rose colored glasses." Dirty Larry says.

Dirty Larry gets excited and looks at the Optician. "Hey! Do you have any rose colored glasses?"

"No I'm afraid we don't sell those here."

Dirty Larry looks around the room. "To bad, if you did you could probably afford a better place."

The Optician takes offense to this. "I'll have you

know I just moved into this place and am still straightening up. I don't see how someone of your hygienic habits has any right to judge."

Super Granny pulls Dirty Larry back and steps in front of him. " I'm sorry and thank you for your time sir."

The Optician composes himself. "That's quite alright, but there is one more thing I need."

The optician steps near Mr. Fix-it and points to an eye chart on the far wall. Now if you will read the lowest line on that chart, we can test how your glasses work."

Mr. Fix-it looks at the chart without strain and reads the lowest line he can see. "Made in China."

The Optician steps up to the chart and can see the small imprint at the bottom That reads: "*Made in China.*" He nods. "They seem to work just fine."

Dirty Larry snarls his nose. "Made in China? What kind of joint are you running here? No wonder I couldn't read that sign, it's in a foreign language and it's probably made by kids who aren't even old enough to spell yet."

The Optician decides he doesn't like this man very well. "We're through here, if you don't mind I have other work to do, good day to you all."

Super Granny nods and smiles, then turns and pushes everyone out the front door.

The parking lot...

Three Gang members are standing in the parking lot near the Senior Gang's van. Scrapper, a rough looking, muscular young Hispanic man in his late teens, is the leader and is acting as look out. Bean Pole, a scrawny Young black boy in his mid teens, is knelt down trying to loosen the lug nuts on a car next to the Seniors van. Skizz, a goofy looking young white boy in his late teens, is helping Bean Pole. Scrapper spots the Senior Gang heading in their direction and motions for his buddies to stop. "Hold up dawgs, we got's us some geezers headed this way."

Bean Pole and Skizz stand up next to Scrapper and watch the Senior Gang approach. "That look like easy money rolling this way, dawg. You gonna step up on them vic's?" Bean Pole asks.

"Fo shizzle." Scrapper says.

The Senior Gang near the van with G.I. in front. Scrapper stops them and Bean Pole and Skizz walk around them on opposite sides and stand behind them. Bean Pole positions himself behind Wild Rose. Skizz positions himself behind Lady Po Po. Scrapper steps in front of G.I. and holds his hand up to stop him. "Hold up Pops. Whats crackalackin'?"

Everyone, except Lady Po Po looks at him very confused. Dirty Larry is the most confused and stares at Scrapper intently with an open mouth. "He just asked whats up." Lady Po Po says.

100

"Not that it's any of your business, but we're gonna get our van and leave." G.I. says.

Scrapper points his finger at G.I. "Don't be dissin' me pops."

Scrapper notices Dirty Larry still staring with an open mouth. "What's you gawkin' at fizzle?"

"He wants to know what that fool is staring at." Lady Po Po says.

Dirty Larry frowns. "Hey! That's not nice."

Cowboy steps up close to Lady Po Po and nudges her with his elbow. "You speak that language?"

Lady Po Po nods. "Had to learn it when I was on Vice Squad."

Scrapper overhears Lady Po Po's response. "Fo Rizzle? Yo five oh?"

Lady Po Po nods again. "I was, I'm retired now."

Scrapper grins. "That piece of four-one-one is gonna cost you extra. Ya see me and my dawgs own this lot, if you want ta park yore ride here you gotta pay. So now you can cough up some bank or bounce on out of here and leave yore ride behind as payment."

G.I., angry, puts his cigar in his mouth, takes a step forward and speaks his mind. "I've had about all I can stand of you, you and your ladies need to step aside and let us through before I give you an attitude adjustment."

101

Scrapper raises his shirt to show a handgun tucked into his waist band. "Ya best stop getting all up in my grill geezer, fo' I take this biscuit and bust a cap in yores."

Lady Po Po starts to translate. "He said..."

G.I. interrupts her before she can finish. "Yea I think I understood that. Let's see if he can understand me."

Scrapper Gets a confused look on his face. "What's you..."

Before Scrapper can finish his question, G.I. lunges forward and grabs the gang bangers nose with one hand and the gun with the other. The gun is still in the gang bangers waist band. Scrapper's eyes water and he can not move from the pain of his nose. Before the other two gang bangers can react, Wild Rose and, Lady Po Po quickly elbow the gang bangers in the stomach and put them in head locks. Dirty Larry and Mr. Fix-it pull Bean Pole's and Skizz's pants down. Wild Rose and Lady Po Po push the two gang bangers to the ground. Cowboy kicks them in the butt and in the most red neck voice he can muster says. "Git on outa' here."

Bean Pole and Skizz stand and run as fast as they can stumbling and tripping on their pants as they try to run and pull them up at the same time. G.I. still has Scrapper by the nose and the gun stuck down his pants. "Looks like your ladies don't love you no more. Now this can go one of two ways. One, I can pull the trigger on what you referred to as a biscuit and blow your other two biscuits off or Two, I can let you go and we can for get the whole thing and you don't bother no one again. Now you answer with a nod the best you can, do you want choice number one?"

Scrapper shakes his head *no* the best he can while G.I. squeezes his nose. G.I. continues. "How about choice number two?"

Scrapper nods his head *yes* the best he can. G.I. pulls the gun out of the gang bangers pants and lets his nose go. "I believe that's a wise choice. If you want to be a big man, you should stop running around causing trouble and go back to school and make something of yourself. Now like my friend Cowboy, told your lady friends, you best git on outa' here."

Scrapper runs off crying and holding his nose. G.I. disassembles the gun and removes the firing pin. He drops the gun parts into a near by trash can and throws the firing pin into some bushes. The Senior Gang continue to the van and get in.

Later...

Scrapper and another gang banger, Bonehead are sitting on the steps of a run down apartment building, Scrapper has a bandaged nose. An old man and woman are walking their dog heading in the direction of the gang bangers. When the couple get close, Bonehead nudges Scrapper with his elbow. "Lookee here it's easy money coming our way."

Scrapper looks up, sees the the elderly couple and gets a fearful look and shakes his head. "No way, there ain't nuthin' easy about old geezers."

As the couple approach, the old man waves at the two gang bangers. "Hello there young fellows."

Scrapper gets up slowly and holds his hands in front of himself. "I don't want no trouble mister, I was just leaving."

Scrapper takes off running as Bonehead calls out to him in confusion. "Hey, where are ya going?"

Scrapper is still running as he answers. "Forget this, I'm through banging, I'm going back ta school"

Bonehead scratches his head in confusion. The old lady waves at Scrapper, as he runs off. "What a nice young man, he must really like school to be in that big a hurry."

Bonehead still has no clue what's going on, he just sits there dumbfounded, as the elderly couple smile at him and continue on their way.

Chapter 9
What a Bunch of Animals

Get-A-Lot...

A large parking lot and huge bulk item store, a sign on top of store reads: "*Get-A-Lot*" in big letters under this, is a smaller sign that reads: "*Get a lot for a little*."

Inside...

The Senior Gang enter the store and stand in awe of it's size. Speed spots some motorized shopping carts in the corner. "Hey, guys lets have some fun."

The Senior Gang all get on motorized shopping carts and start zooming down the isles. Dirty Larry bumps into Speed and this starts a game of bumper cars. Speed bumps Dirty Larry, who slams into a stack of toilet paper, that collapses on top of him. Dirty Larry backs up and quickly tries to catch up. Super Granny slams into G.I., knocking him into a

105

pole, the jolt knocks G.I.'s false teeth out. He grabs them off the floor wipes them off, before putting them in his mouth and gives chase.

Two security guards spot the commotion. Berry, a potbellied slob with a wrinkled untucked uniform and Bentley, a very skinny lazy looking nerd, both give chase on foot. Speed sees the security guards and smiles as he motions for the Senior Gang to follow him. Speed is enjoying the ride as he slides around a corner. "Whoo hoo hoo hoooo."

The two security guards cannot keep up, by the time they reach the end of the isle, the Senior Gang are gone. As the two security guards are looking down the isle, the Senior Gang cross the isle behind them, With Speed in the lead. "Whoo hoo hoo hoooo."

The security guards run to the other isle and again it's to late. The Senior Gang cross the isle behind them once again. "Whoo hoo hoo hoooo."

The two guards scratch their head in confusion and both are to tired to run anymore. Berry is breathing so hard he can't even speak, he points to Bentley's Radio and sits on the floor. Bentley is gasping for air also, but manages to talk into his radio's microphone. "Code red, code red in section forty-four, release the mobile unit."

An overhead door raises on the back wall and four security guards ride out on *Segways*, the two wheeled motorized scooters. The four guards, with flashing lights and sirens, chase the Senior Gang. Speed spots them and slows down enough to let the rest of the Senior Gang pass him. Speed does a power slide and spins around to face the guards and stops in the middle of the isle. The Senior Gang stop and watch Speed. The guards stop their Segways, one guards motions for the rest to shut off the sirens. After the sirens are off the guard picks up his microphone and speaks over a loud speaker. "The fun's over, step off of the carts and walk toward us."

There is no response from the Senior Gang. The guard continues. "If you do not comply with my orders we will be forced to use drastic measures."

Speed smiles and takes off, only Speed could get a motorized shopping cart to spin it's wheels and burn rubber. The guards take off, lined up and heading straight for Speed. Speed and the Segway guards plays chicken, but Speed ain't no a chicken. The two middle guards swerve out of the way and crash. Speed does another power slide and chases the other two Segway guards. The hunters are now the hunted. The two guards are so scared they can't keep from looking back at Speed and crash into each other and spin out of control.

The two guards watch in a daze as Speed races by. "Whoo hoo hoo hoooo."

The Senior Gang raise their hands and Speed high fives them as he passes. The rest of the Senior

107

Gang fall in behind Speed and they all continue to race down the isles. As the Senior Gang reach the middle of the isle, multiple security guards in full riot gear rush out and block the Senior Gang from both ends of the isle. The Senior Gang stop and ponder the situation. Speed smiles big and prepares to take off, but before he can Super Granny pulls up beside him and places her hand on his shoulder. "I know you can get by them and it's been fun, but this may get us into more trouble than it's worth."

Speed nods, he thinks it would be real fun, but he knows Super Granny is right, people don't take this to lightly in this day and age.

Later...

The Senior Gang stumble out the front doors as they are shoved out by the security guards in riot gear. Berry steps up to the door. "And stay out, I'm gonna post your photos all over the store if you ever come back we're gonna have you arrested and prosecuted to the fullest extent of the law."

The Senior Gang look at each other then start to laugh and head for the van in the parking lot.

Later...

The Senior Gang walk through the front entrance of a zoo. A large sign over the entrance reads: "*Bomar County Zoo.*" Various people of all walks of life are waiting to get in. As they each go through the rotary bars, Dirty Larry gets stuck and can't make the bars move. Wild Rose walks up behind him and gives him a hard shove. The bar gives and Dirty Larry stumbles through barley keeping his balance. "Thanks Rose."

Wild Rose winks."Glad to oblige."

Inside...

The Senior Gang's first stop is the elephant cages. Dirty Larry stands next to the edge and uses his arm like a trunk and tries to make elephant noises. One of the elephants gets trunk full of water and soaks Dirty Larry with one massive spray. The rest of the Senior Gang flinch and laugh as the water impacts and splashes on them. Dirty Larry gets a mad look on his face. "It ain't been a year yet, that's twice this month someone gave me a bath. What's your problem elephant? Don't make me come down there."

The elephant gets another trunk full of water and Dirty Larry quickly walks away. On the way to the next exhibit, Dirty Larry rummages through a trashcan and finds a half eaten corn dog. He takes a bite then offers a bite to the rest of the Senior Gang, Who snarl their noses and walk away. Dirty Larry shrugs shoulders and takes another bite, then quickly catches up.

At the camel pens, Dirty Larry stands face to face with a camel and they both stare at each other while chewing the same way. The camel tires of this and spits a big glob of white goo in Dirty Larry's face. Dirty Larry calmly wipes the goo off of his face and spits in the camels face. The camel stumbles, turns and runs away. Dirty Larry rushes up to the edge of the pen. "Yea, you better run away, you can dish it out, but you can't take it. Come back here you coward, we just got started."

Dirty Larry continues to rant as G.I. grabs him by the arm and pulls him along with the rest of the Senior Gang. The next stop is the orangutan habitat, Cowboy points his finger at an orangutan and the orangutan sticks his hands in the air. Cowboy lowers his finger and the orangutan lowers his arms. Everybody laughs, Cowboy points his finger at the orangutan and the orangutan sticks his arms in the air, cowboy lowers his finger and the orangutan lowers his arms each time. Cowboy and the orangutan do this several times. "He's so cute." Lady Po Po says.

"yea, we are ta' take the little fella with us." Cowboy says.

G.I. points at Dirty Larry. "We already got a stinky, little hairy fella."

Dirty Larry frowns, then smells his left underarm, then the right, shrugs and smiles. The Senior Gang laugh and continue on their way. As they pass the bear cage a big grizzly stands on his hind legs and lets out a ferocious roar at the

Seniors. Everyone, but Wild Rose nearly jump out of their skin. Wild Rose walks up close, raises her hands and snarls back, the bear drops to all fours, turns and walks away. Super Granny smiles."I guess that bear didn't want to tangle with Wild Rose."

"Smart bear." Lady Po Po says.

When the Senior Gang reach the sea lion exhibit, they stop and watch a graceful display by the sea lions. Dirty Larry stands up on a near by rock and does a short ballerina type dance. The sea lions all line up on a bank of rocks below and clap their front flippers together and bark, as though they are applauding for his performance. Dirty Larry bows and blows kisses to his new fans.

Later...

At an inside chimpanzee viewing area, the Senior Gang are looking at the chimps through a glass partition. All the Senior Gang look tired and worn out from the fun they have had at the zoo. Dirty Larry starts imitating the actions of one of the chimpanzees. The chimp doesn't seem to like this much and flings his poo toward the glass partition and it hits with a thud. Everyone except Dirty Larry flinches and runs backward. Dirty Larry continues to stare like he's intrigued. Super Granny throws up her hands. "Okay that's it, I believe I've seen all I want to see at the zoo, lets

111

get out of here."

The Senior Gang turn and walk toward the exit. Dirty Larry talks as they walk. "Hey guys did you know that monkeys been eating corn? Did you know they fed them corn? Hey is anyone else hungry for corn?"

At a restaurant...

The Senior Gang is sitting at a table in a restaurant, looking at menus. Stephanie Smith, an attractive, fit looking waitress in her late twenties, walks over to take their order. "Are you folks ready to order or do you need a few more minutes?"

Super Granny looks up and smiles at Stephanie. "I think we're ready, We all decided to have the special."

Stephanie writes the order down. "Specials all around that's easy enough."

Stephanie starts to walk away, but Dirty Larry stops her. "Wait. Does the special have corn?"

Stephanie looks on the menu. "Yes sir it does."

"Good cause for some reason I'm hungry for corn."

Super Granny shakes her head, Stephanie starts to turn away once more, but again Dirty Larry stops her. "Wait. They call me Dirty Larry, because I look and sound like "Dirty Harry", I want to do something."

Dirty Larry squints his eyes and in a very bad Clint Eastwood as Dirty Harry impression says. "Go ahead lady make my special."

Dirty Larry excitedly looks at Stephanie. "See didn't that sound just like him?"

Stephanie, confused politely smiles back at him. "Yes sir, that's quite a talent you have."

G.I. kicks Dirty Larry in the leg under the table. Dirty Larry flinches and grabs his leg as he gives G.I. a mean look. Super Granny shakes her head then embarrassingly looks at Stephanie. "Sorry about that, thank you."

Stephanie is amused and smiles. "Yes ma'am, I'll have your order right out."

Stephanie turns and walks away. Dirty Larry is still giving G.I. a mean look. "What did you kick me for?

"To get you to stop making a fool out of yourself. People call you Dirty Larry because your name is Larry and your dirty, not cause you look or sound like Dirty Harry. You don't look or sound anything like him."

"Dirty Larry raises his eyebrows and weaves his head in an arrogant motion. "Oh, like your some kind of expert on Dirty Harry. Well I look and sound like him more than you do."

G.I. chuckles. "Well if your Dirty Harry, I guess that makes me the Six Million Dollar Man."

Dirty Larry responds in a loud voice. "Ha, you

113

wish."

The other patrons are now staring at the two arguing. Super Granny notices and tries to settle them down. "Would you two stop, your in public stop arguing and use your inside voice. I can't take you two anywhere. Everyone is staring, have a little manners and try and act sophisticated."

G.I. ducks his head. "Sorry, your right."

"Yea me too." Dirty Larry says.

Both men shake hands and forgive each other. Dirty Larry looks confused. "I didn't quite understand that last part, sufi...sufisti..."

'Sophisticated." Lady Po Po says.

Dirty Larry points at Lady Po Po. "Yea what she said."

"It means your in a fancy restaurant so act accordingly." Super Granny says.

Dirty Larry gets a look as though he understands. "Oh, why didn't you say so in the first place?"

Dirty Larry picks up a cracker on the table and holds it with his pinkie finger out likeHe's trying to be fancy and takes a bite. He turns to see a fancy woman staring at him, so he opens his mouth and shows her the chewed cracker. The woman quickly turns back around and stops staring. Dirty Larry smiles and turns to see, Super Granny shaking her head at him. Dirty Larry ducks his head and shrugs his shoulders.

Chapter 10
A Skip and a Chase

After eating, the Senior Gang all look full and satisfied. Dirty Larry leans back in his chair and rubs his belly. "That was good, we ought to eat like that more often."

"If we ate like that more often we'd all be to big to get around." G.I. says.

Stephanie walks over to the Seniors table and lays the bill on the table. "I'll be your cashier when your ready."

As Stephanie walks away, Super Granny picks the bill up and sets it in front of Wild Rose. Wild Rose looks in her purse, then gets a scared look on her face, as she looks at Super Granny. "It's gone."

Super Granny doesn't understand. "What?"

Wild Rose is almost in a panic, which is very unlike her. "The money, it's gone, we spent it all."

Super Granny starts doing the math in her head. "The eight hundred at the carnival, the eye doctor,

115

the glasses, the zoo, oh no, we did spend it all."

Wild Rose gets even more nervous. "What are we gonna do?"

Super Granny pats Wild Rose's hand. "Calm down, panicking isn't going to help us, let's think it over, I'm sure we can come up with a solution."

Speed leans in and whispers. "I think we're gonna have ta sneak out and come back and pay them when we get more money."

Super Granny frowns. "I don't like sneaking out on a bill, but Speed's right we don't have much choice, we'll just have to pay them later. Does everyone agree or does someone have a better idea?"

G.I. puts his cigar in his mouth. "I'm in."

"Yea, we can come back and pay later." Lady Po Po says.

Dirty Larry smiles excitedly. "Let's do it."

"I can't think of any better plan, I'm in too." Mr. Fix-it says.

Wild Rose doesn't say a word, she simply nods her head in agreement. Cowboy tugs on the front of his hat. "I'm game, lets posse up and get this done."

The Senior Gang slowly stand up and start sneaking toward the exit, They are all hunched over and tip toeing toward the exit. They believe no one notices them, but they are just drawing attention. Everyone in the restaurant is staring at them. As they approach the entrance they hear someone clear his throat and ask. "Where do you people think your going?"

The Senior Gang all look up to see, the Restaurant Manager, a short, nerdy looking man in his early twenties, blocking their path. Cowboy stands up straight and pushes his hat up. "I reckon we was headed for the exit before ya so rudely interrupted us."

The Manager folds his arms in front of his chest. "What about your bill?"

"What bill?" Speed asks.

"The one that was brought to your table for all the food you ate."

Speed smiles. "Oh, that bill, well there's a funny story about that."

The Manager is not amused. "I bet there is."

Dirty Larry acts like he's chocking, the Manager doesn't buy it. "That won't work you didn't even have any food in your mouth."

Dirty Larry grabs his stomach and acts like he's getting sick and looks up at the Manager. The Manager shakes his head. Dirty Larry straightens up and looks up like he's thinking hard, then looks at the manager and says. "Um, my dog ate it?"

The Manager shakes his head. "Your trying to walk out without paying."

"Now wait, we're a little short of cash, but we were planning on coming back to pay the bill."

Speed says.

"Your all nothing, but a bunch of trashy thieves." The Manager says.

G.I. takes offense to this. He knows his friends and he knows that none of them, with the exception of Dirty Larry, are trashy. He also knows that none of them, including Dirty Larry, are thieves. He steps forward ready to lay into the Manager. "Now hold it right there mister, I won't let you talk that way."

Super Granny grabs G.I.'s arm. "Hold on G.I., you can't solve every problem with violence."

"It always worked in the past." G.I. says.

Super Granny smiles. "Yea, but times change."

G.I. ducks his head in disappointment, he knows Super Granny is right, but he doesn't like it. Stephanie is now behind the Senior Gang trying to see whats going on. The Manager points his finger at the Senior Gang. "I think I'll call the police and have all of you throwed in jail."

Dirty Larry gets a fearful look about him. "I don't want to go to the poky, I'm to pretty. Do you know what they do to pretty boys like me in jail?"

Stephanie reaches into her pocket and pulls out her tip money and steps forward. "Don't worry, um, it was Dirty Larry Right?"

Dirty Larry nods. "Yes ma'am."

Stephanie pats Dirty Larry on the back. "Well Dirty Larry don't worry."

Stephanie steps up to the Manager. "I have their money right here."

Stephanie counts out enough money to pay the bill and a tip and hands it to him. "Keep the change."

The Manager looks at the Senior Gang. "I want you people out of here, now."

He points his finger at Stephanie. "You can go with them."

Super Granny steps forward. "Now wait a..."

"It's okay ma'am I'm tired of working for this peon anyway, always trying to push his authority around because he's such a small man in both body and mind." Stephanie says.

This infuriates the Manager and he points to the exit. "Get out now, all of you."

The Senior Gang walk out the front door and Stephanie walks out with them.

Outside...

The Senior Gang are standing just outside the entrance talking to Stephanie. "Thank you for what you did for us in there, we'll pay you the money back, but I'm sorry it cost you your job." Super Granny says.

Stephanie smiles. "Don't worry about it I didn't lose much. Besides I have a little money set aside that I'd like to invest in my own business, I just got to figure out what that is."

"Do you have a car or a ride?" Lady Po Po asks.

"I rode to work with one of the other girls, I'll just have to wait around here until she gets off work." Stephanie says.

Dirty Larry speaks up. "She could go with us."

Super Granny smiles. "He's right we can take you anywhere you need to go."

Stephanie shakes her head. "No, I don't want to be a bother."

"It's no bother, we have plenty of room and it's the least we can do." Super Granny says.

Stephanie smiles and nods. " Okay, I don't have any particular place I need to be right now, but if you can stand the company, I think I'd enjoy riding around with you folks."

Super Granny puts her hand on Stephanie's shoulder. "We'd all love to have you."

Everyone nods in agreement. "Welcome aboard ma'am." Speed says.

Stephanie smiles, she knows that she could not be in any better company and is looking forward to the trip. "Thank you."

Cowboy tugs on the front of his hat. "Lets saddle up and ride."

Wild Rose is not ready to leave just yet. "Wait. Um, I better go back in and go to the bathroom first."

It's not quite the truth, but she doesn't want anyone trying to stop her. "Okay Rose take your time we'll wait on you." Super Granny says.

Wild Rose smiles and heads back into the restaurant. Stephanie and the rest of the Senior Gang wait for her.

Inside...

Wild Rose enters the restaurant and heads straight for the Manager. The Manager turns to see her approaching. "What are you doing back in here, I told you..."

Before he can finish his statement, Wild Rose grabs the manager by the shirt with both hands and lifts him off the ground. "I came back to talk to you little man. You need to know if you ever treat my friends like that again I'll rip you into pieces. Do we understand each other?"

The Manager is so terrified that he can't even form a coherent word. "Ye...ye...ye..."

The Manager is almost in tears when liquid runs out his pants leg and puddles on the floor. Wild Rose puts him back down and turns loose of his shirt, when she sees the puddle. "I'll take that as a yes. Me and my friends aren't thieves and you best not call us that again, in fact you best treat all my friends with respect."

The other waitresses are watching and some start to giggle. The Manager's face turns three shades of red, he tries to turn his embarrassment into anger. "What are you laughing at, I'll fire all of you."

Wild Rose just won't tolerate it, she points to the waitresses. "Those ladies are my friends too."

The Manager burst into tears and runs bawling toward the front doors. Everyone in the restaurant starts to clap. Wild Rose smiles and nods then calmly heads for the doors.

Outside...

The front doors slam open and the Manager, still bawling hysterically, runs past the Senior Gang and Stephanie. All watch in confusion, as the Manager runs away. Dirty Larry points at the Manager running away. "See, I'm not the only one that makes people cry when I go to the bathroom."

Wild Rose walks out of the restaurant and over to the group. "What was all of that about Rose?" Super Granny asks.

Wild Rose looks at G.I. and smiles. "Well let's just say that times may change, but some folks just want to stay the same."

G.I. smiles at Wild Rose, winks and nods. The group turns and heads for the van.

A short distance away...

A police cruiser is parked on the side of the street near the restaurant parking lot. Sitting inside the police cruiser are Pete "Pete" Fletcher, an experienced looking officer in his mid forties and

Pete "Re-Pete" Simpson, a young rookie in his early twenties. They have been partnered up for six months now. They have been given the nicknames of Pete and Re-Pete, both sit watching traffic go by. Pete spots the Senior Gang getting in their van and points them out to his partner. "Look at that eight seniors fitting the description of the APB we got this morning."

"You think it's the same ones?" Re-Pete asks.

Pete gives his rookie partner a funny look. "How many groups of eight seniors that exactly match that description do you think there are in this city?"

Re-Pete ducks his head in embarrassment. Then both officers watch as the Senior Gang's van pulls out of the parking lot and onto the street. Pete slaps his partner on the shoulder. "Light em' up."

Pete puts the cruiser in gear and pulls out behind the Senior Gang's van. Re-Pete flips a switch to turn on the flashing lights.

Inside van...

Mr. Fix-it, who is now sitting in back, notices the flashing lights. "Speed we got company back here."

Speed looks in the rear view mirror and smiles. "Just like old times, everyone buckle up and hang on tight, we're about ta have us some fun."

Speed steps on the gas pedal pushing it to the

123

floor. The van speeds down the streets as the Cruiser gives chase. Both vehicles power slide around corners, dart in and out of traffic, cut through alleys and ram through fences.

Inside the cruiser...

Re-Pete is holding on to the roof strap with one hand and the dash with the other, but he's enjoying the chase. "Does he really think he can get away?"

Pete jerks the wheel to take another corner then addresses his partner. "Boy, you better learn something real quick, don't ever underestimate an old timer, experience counts for a lot."

Re-Pete nods. "Yes sir."

Pete Braces himself as the cruiser rumbles over a curb, after the ride smooths out he continues to speak to his partner. "You can't teach an old dog new tricks, but they already know a lot of old tricks and some of them still have some bite left in them."

"What about this one?" Re-Pete asks.

Pete Smiles. "Well, I don't know who he is, but judging from the way he's driving, I'd say he's got a lot of bite and you better hang on tight cause we're in for a wild ride."

Both vehicles slam through a fence and emerge on a gravel road that runs along the rail road tracks. The two vehicles are now speeding along side a fast moving train that has one flat car in the middle.

Inside van...

The Senior Gang are all very calm as though it was a leisurely Sunday drive. Stephanie, however is wide eyed and terrified and is holding on for dear life. Super Granny notices Stephanie and pats her on the hand and tries to reassure her. "It's okay Stephanie, Speed knows exactly what he's doing."

Speed looks over to see the flat car on the train, then he looks forward in the distance, he squints to make out a pile of dirt and smiles. "Y'all better hold on tighter than you ever held on before."

"What do you have in mind Speed?" G.I. asks.

Speed points to the train. "Ya see that flat car on the train?"

G.I. nods. "Yes sir."

Speed points to the dirt pile in the distance. "Ya see that pile of dirt up there?"

G.I. nods again. "Yes sir."

Speed looks at G.I. and smiles. "Nuff said."

G.I. smiles, takes the cigar out of his mouth and secures it in his pocket, then he looks back. "You heard him you all better hang on as tight as you can."

The Senior Gang brace themselves. Stephanie is still holding on for dear life and now grips even tighter. The van hits the dirt pile and goes air born, in midair we can hear Speed from inside the van.

125

"Whooo hoo hoo hooo."

The van flies over the flat car of the train and lands safely on the other side. The police cruiser power slides sideways and slams into the dirt pile.

Inside the cruiser...

Both Police Officers are sitting in the cruiser with dirty faces and dust flying all around. Pete spits dirt out of his mouth. "Some old dogs have more bite than others."

Inside van...

Everyone is now both excited and relieved. Their excitement fades to worry and disappointment when they look up to see a road block in front of them and behind them. Speed shakes his head. "I miss the old days."

G.I. points to a side road. "Hey there's a construction yard over there, pull in there and buy us some time to think."

Chapter 11
Senior Gang to the Rescue

Several blocks away...

Danny's car is traveling along the city streets. Danny and Sherrie are arguing when Danny's cellphone rings. Danny answers the phone. "Hello...Yes sir...Yes sir I know where it's at...Okay thank you sir I'll be right there."

Danny hangs up and puts the cellphone away. "That was the police department, they found mom and her friends, they have them blocked in at McPearson's construction yard."

Later...

Danny pulls up to the construction site's entrance, that is blocked and barricaded by the police. Phil Booth, now a Police Captain in his late sixties with an average build, is standing by the barricade, he approaches the drivers side of Danny's car. Danny rolls down his window. Phil

127

bends down a bit so he can see the whole interior of the car. He checks the back and looks at Sherrie, then Danny, when he's satisfied that it is safe he speaks. "Sorry folks, we have a situation inside and I can't let you in."

"Officer, my mom is one of the seniors inside, her name is Grace Hudson." Danny says.

Phil nods sympathetically. "It's Captain sir, Captain Phil Booth and..."

Phil stops mid sentence when he recognizes the name. "Did you say Grace Hudson?"

Danny nods. "Yes sir, uh Captain."

Phil smiles. "You wouldn't be Danny would you?"

Danny is surprised and taken off guard that he knows him. "Yes sir that's me, how did you know?"

Phil lets out a little laugh before he answers. "I'm one of the officers that dropped you off at Mrs. Hudson's home for troubled teens, you sure were a wild one back then, looks like Mrs. Hudson raised you right."

Danny smiles and nods. "Yes sir, she was the only one that cared about me, she taught me about respect, manners and everything else I needed. I remember you, the best thing that ever happened to me was when you and your partner dropped me off with her."

Phil pauses in thought. Being a cop is a

thankless job. It sometimes seems as though you are just spinning your wheels and getting nowhere. You arrest a perp only to have them released by the courts and start the process over again. It's moments like these that make everything worth while and restores your faith in the system. Phil snaps back to reality and smiles. "I'm glad it worked out, I like to hear when something we do works. Here's what I'm gonna do, I'm gonna call off the officers inside, their not doing much good anyway just going in circles, literally, anyway I'll call them off and let you through and you try to talk them down and let's end this before someone gets hurt."

Danny nods. "Thank you sir."

Phil pats on the door, then while talking on his radio, walks to the barricade and moves it enough for Danny to drive through.

The center of the construction site...

The Senior Gang's van is doing donuts in the gravel and stirring up dust. Two police cruisers are trying to chase with lights and sirens blaring. The two police cruisers turn off their lights and sirens and drive away. The Senior Gang watch the cruisers leave. Dirty Larry gets excited. "Hey they left, they must have realized it was no use and quit."

G.I. shakes his head, then points to Danny's

approaching car. "No that wasn't it, look there's another car pulling in."

Lady Po Po looks out the window as though she recognizes the car. "Super Granny isn't that Danny's car?"

Super Granny nods with a concerned look on her face. "Yes it is, Speed stop the van I'm going to go talk to him."

Speed stops the van, Danny pulls up close to the van and stops, Danny puts the car in park. "I'm gonna go talk to mom, you wait in the car."

Sherrie rolls her eyes arrogantly and looks out the passenger window. As Danny steps out Sherrie throws her purse on the console and unknowingly knocks the gear shift into reverse. Super Granny and Danny hug each other. Danny grabs Super Granny by the shoulders and gently pushes her away a little with a concerned look. "Mom, What is going on?"

Danny looks over to see Stephanie, Stephanie looks back. "Um Hi." Danny says.

Stephanie is a bit bashful and answers quietly. "Hi."

Super Granny smiles. "Danny this is Stephanie. Stephanie this is my son Danny."

Stephanie is no longer bashful, Super Granny has told her so much about him that she feels as though they are old friends. "Oh He's the one you've been telling me about."

Stephanie steps toward Danny with her hand extended. "I feel like I already know..."

Stephanie's statement is cut short by Sherrie's panicked screams. "Help, someone help me."

Everyone looks to see the car rolling backward. It rolls down a hill and knocks out a post under an over hanging structure, which starts to wobble and threatens to come crashing down. The car continues to roll into a sewage lagoon and floats to the middle and slowly starts to sink. Danny starts to panic. "Oh god, oh god, oh my god."

Super Granny grabs Danny by the shirt collar and slaps him. Danny's panic turns to surprise. "Mom?"

"Sorry Danny it had to be done, now get a hold of yourself, panicking isn't going to accomplish anything." Super Granny says.

Danny composes himself and nods. "Yes ma'am."

Super Granny takes charge of the situation and starts coordinating the rescue. She points to a cable laying on the ground. "Cowboy do you think you can use that cable like a rope and rope something on that car?"

Cowboy pulls his hat down tight. "Yes ma'am."

"Then get it done." Super Granny says.

Cowboy grabs the cable and quickly heads for the car. Super Granny motions to Wild Rose. "Rose you put some muscle in it and help Cowboy hold that car until speed can get backed up there."

Wild Rose doesn't hesitate, she answers while running. "Yes ma'am."

Super Granny points to the van and looks at Speed. "Speed get the van and put the hitch as close to them as you can."

Speed runs for the van. "I'm on it."

Super Granny points at the teetering structure. "Mr. Fix-it you cut a brace to put under that structure before it crashes down on top of them."

Mr. Fix-it looks around and spots a pile of posts with a hand saw laying on top of them. "Consider it done Super Granny."

Mr. Fix-it runs to a pile of posts. Super Granny looks at G.I. "G.I. do you have a military knot or hitch that you can fasten that cable to the van with?"

G.I. nods. "Yes ma'am I do."

"Then get that mission done soldier." Super Granny says.

G.I. smiles. "HOOAH."

G.I. charges to his objective and quickly puts his cigar in his mouth along the way. Near the sewage lagoon, Cowboy lassos the front tire with the cable and pulls tight. Wild Rose grabs the cable and pulls hard, the car lurches back out a noticeable amount and then holds study. G.I. works the cable into a bowline knot, Speed drives up and power slides the van all the way around to put the ball hitch in just the right place, G.I places the cable over the hitch. All of this is done smoothly and precisely.

The structure overhead teeters more and threatens to come tumbling down. Mr. Fix-it, with tongue out holds up his thumb and closes one eye as to measure the distance between the teetering structure and the ground, he then swings his thumb over to the post, grabs the saw and saws off a post. Mr. Fix-it grabs the long post and slings it over his shoulder, then quickly carries it to the structure and puts it in place, a perfect fit. The structure is now stable. Everyone relaxes and lets out a sigh of relief.

Danny watches the actions of the Senior Gang with amazement and surprise. Super Granny Grabs Dirty Larry by the shoulders and looks him in the eyes. "Dirty Larry your the only one who'd be willing to do what needs doing next, but I hate to ask."

Dirty Larry is so excited he's shaking his legs. "Put me in coach."

Super Granny smiles proudly. "Okay, do you think you can swim out there and help her back to land?"

Dirty Larry can't hardly contain his excitement. "I thought you'd never ask."

Dirty Larry runs for the lagoon, without

stopping Dirty Larry does a swan dive into the lagoon. He comes up doing the backstroke and spitting water out his mouth like he's out for a leisurely swim in a pool. He swims over to the car and taps on the passenger side window. "You need to open the door and come with me ma'am."

Sherrie shakes her head furiously. "I'm not getting in that filth."

Dirty Larry taps on the window again. "You don't really have an option ma'am, one way or another your gonna be in this filth. You can get out and swim through this filth to safety or you can stay in there and drowned in this filth, because this cars not gonna stay up much longer."

The car bubbles and drops a bit starting to sink. Sherrie reluctantly opens the door with the help of Dirty Larry. Sherrie gets on Dirty Larry's back and wraps her arms around his neck. Dirty Larry dog paddles back to dry land. The rest of the Senior Gang, Danny and Stephanie are all waiting and help them out of the sewage. Danny is still amazed at how the Senior Gang handled the situation. "Wow that was amazing, you guys did great, I'm shocked."

Super Granny steps closer to Danny and smiles. "Why, did you think we were just a bunch of senile old geezers that couldn't take care of ourselves, much less help out in an emergency?"

Danny lowers his head in shame. "Well, um,

well yea I guess I did."

Super Granny looks at him, she is both surprised and disappointed. "Danny, I taught you better than that, I taught you to never judge anyone."

Danny droops his head even further. "I know mom and I'm sorry."

Super Granny shakes her head. "I can still function just fine, I don't belong in a nursing home, none of us do. We're not drooling and pooping ourselves yet."

Danny raises his head just a little. "I know mom, it's just that everything that was happening..."

"I did it." Sherrie says

Danny doesn't understand what she means. "What?"

Sherrie Doesn't want to admit anything, but even the most self centered witch can have their moments of honesty. "Everything you put her in the nursing home for, I did it. The milk in the cabinet, the misplaced keys, everything, I did it. I wanted her out of the house."

Danny's shame turns to surprise. "What about the gas on the stove being left on?"

"That was me too." Sherrie says.

Danny's surprise turns to guilt as he looks at Super Granny. "I'm sorry mom, I should have never doubted you, I knew better."

Super Granny smiles and nods to let him know she forgives him. Danny's guilt turns to anger as he turns to face Sherrie. "All this time you never put any effort into our relationship and now I find out you been trying to destroy my family. Who was next Jimmy?"

Sherrie tries to speak. "I'm..."

Danny knows from the look on Sherrie's face, her moment of honesty has came and went. He knows the next thing that comes out of her mouth is likely to be a lie, He holds up his hand to stop her from talking. "I don't want to hear it, just get out of my site I don't want anything to do with you ever again."

Sherrie's act of remorse quickly fades to real anger. "Fine, I don't need you anyway."

Sherrie stomps off, heading toward the entrance. Danny turns his attention back to the seniors. "Now your in trouble with the law for breaking out of some place you never should have been in, in the first place and it's my fault."

Super Granny shakes her head. "No, that's not your fault, as far as the law is concerned we have to take the blame for that ourselves."

Super Granny knows that as far as the law is concerned, they have one last hope. Super Granny is ashamed to even ask such a thing, but it's the only way. "Lady Po Po do you think you have any pull left with the police?"

Lady Po Po shrugs. "I don't know, Danny do you know who's in charge down there?"

"Yes ma'am he said his name was Phil Booth, Captain Phil Booth. He was one of the officers that dropped me off with you mom."

Super Granny remembers him fondly, as she nods and smiles. "I remember him. Do you know him Lady Po Po?"

Lady Po Po smiles from ear to ear. "I've known Phil since he was a rookie and as a matter of fact he owes me a huge favor and I *reckon* now is a good time to collect it."

Super Granny notices the use of a certain word that is not normal for Lady Po Po and calls her on it. "Reckon?"

Lady Po Po grins, as she realizes the word just came out naturally. "I guess Speed, Cowboy and Wild Rose are starting to rub off on me, I'm starting to talk like them now."

Super Granny grins back. "Their rubbing off on me too."

Lady Po Po looks around at everyone and winks. "That's not such a bad thing, good friends are hard to come by and here we go again..."

Lady Po Po pulls her chin back and speaks in the most red neck voice she can manage. "I reckon we got us some good in's."

Super Granny conjures up her own red neck drawl. "I reckon so, now why don't you mosey on

137

down ta that police barricade and do some jawing with the law."

Everyone laughs, Lady Po Po grabs the cigar out of G.I.'s mouth and puts it in her own and heads for the police barricade, at the front entrance. Everyone is still laughing, when Super Granny looks at Dirty Larry. "Now I believe we need to find a hose, because someones going to need a hosing down before they can get in the van."

Dirty Larry gets a worried look on his face. "Not me, I done had enough baths this week. One at the home, the elephant at the zoo gave me a second and that lagoon counts as three, I can't tolerate anymore."

Super Granny scrunches her nose. "I'm being lenient by letting you count the elephant, but that lagoon stinks and it doesn't count as a bath."

Dirty Larry wrings out his shirt tail and filthy water splashes to the ground. "It's wet, so it counts."

Mr. Fix-it motions to the rest of the Gang. "Lets get him."

Everyone starts chasing Dirty Larry around the construction site.

Later...
Just down the street from McPearson's Construction yard, Sherrie is standing on the

corner trying to get a ride. Her hair is nasty and matted, she is filthy and stinks to high heaven. A car pulls up and stops, inside is a sleazy looking man. He rows down the passenger window, Sherrie leans into the window. "How bout a ride mister."

The sleazy man gets a little whiff of the smell. "Gawd almighty, I hope your cheap, cause you don't smell none to good. For the right price I might try ta bare it."

Sherrie looks confused. "What are you talking..."

Before she can finish an unmarked patrol car pulls up behind and flashes it's lights and shortly blares the siren. Phil steps out of the drivers side of the patrol car and approaches Sherrie. "Step away from the vehicle miss."

Sherrie steps back and Phil bends down a little to address the driver. "I got your tag number mister, don't let me catch you around here again, now get going."

The sleazy man doesn't hesitate and quickly drives away. Phil turns and looks at Sherrie. "This is no kind of life ma'am, just look at what it's done to you already. You could get hurt or get some kind of disease or worse."

The wind shifts and Phil gets a whiff of the odor. "Oh my god, from the smell of it you already got some kind of terrible disease. I'm taking you in for your own good ma'am, put you hands against the wall."

Sherrie finally realizes what everyone has been thinking. "No you don't understand it's not like that."

Phil shakes his head. " I've heard it all before lady, now assume the position, or am I going to have to call for backup."

Sherrie is both fearful and furious. "Now wait, you can't, come on you have to believe me, I'm not..."

Sherrie sees that Phil is not buying a word she says, so she gives up and starts bawling as Phil places the cuffs on her wrists.

Chapter 12
Better With Age

Six months later...

A huge, beautiful house on a large acreage just outside of the Bomar City limits. A big sign out front reads: "*Dignity House assisted living.*" in large letters, under this in smaller letters it reads: "*Where mature adults can live with dignity, honor and respect.*"

Inside...

A very large foyer, with a reception desk facing the door and a staircase behind it. Stephanie is sitting at the reception desk talking to an elderly man and his daughter. The elderly man is Ethan Trevor, a slightly short, but very fit elderly man in his seventies. The daughter is Emily Trevor, a short, petite woman in her late thirties. The Senior Gang are sitting behind Stephanie. Jimmy is sitting in Super Granny's lap. Danny walks down the

141

stairs and gives Stephanie a light, quick kiss. "Hi honey."

Stephanie gets a warm feeling, the feeling you get that makes it seem everything is right with the world. "Hi. This is my husband Danny. Danny this is Ethan and Emily Trevor, Mr. Trevor is thinking about staying with us."

Danny smiles and nods to both of them. "Hello sir, ma'am its a pleasure to meet you both."

Ethan and Emily smile and nod back. Danny squeezes Stephanie's shoulders. "Don't let me interrupt you, go ahead and tell them about this place and the staff."

"Okay, Lets start with transportation. We have a large van that can take the residents anywhere they want to go and the driver is the absolute best." Stephanie says.

As she speaks she can clearly see the reality of it in her mind.

Dignity House drive way...

The Senior Gang's van is parked in the drive way and elderly people are getting in.

Inside van...

Speed is in the drivers seat ready to go. One of the passengers is Marge, who sits in the seat behind Speed and reaches up and taps him on the shoulder. "I'm going to be late for my beauty appointment, I have to look good for Cowboy."

Speed leans over until he can see her out of the rear view mirror. "Don't worry ma'am no one is late on my watch, y'all just buckle up, hang on and get ready for some fun."

Speed steps on the gas, throwing everyone back in their seat, as the van takes off. The elderly people inside all start whooping and hollering. A police cruiser is sitting on the shoulder of the road at the end of the Dignity House's long driveway.

Inside the cruiser...

Pete and Re-Pete, the same officers that chased the Senior Gang when they jumped the train, are sitting and waiting. Pete takes a deep breath and lets it out. "I wander why they wanted us to sit way out here? There's nothing going on."

Just then the van zooms past the front of the cruiser and the numbers on the dash radar rapidly count up and stop at ninety five. Re-Pete's mouth drops open. "Hey, wasn't that..."

Both officers look at each other surprised. Pete shakes his head. "Oh Lord here we go again. Hit the lights kid and call it in."

Inside van...

Speed looks in his rear view mirror and sees the cruiser chasing him with lights blaring, he smiles and steps on the gas. "Just like I said this here is

143

where the fun starts, whoo hoo hoo hoooo, just like old times."

Now - Henry "Speed" Jackson - Dignity House Transporter

Stephanie continues to describe the staff and services of Dignity House. "We have a terrific staff and a great manager who keeps the entire staff in line, she's strict, but fair."

Again as she speaks she can clearly see the reality of her story in her mind.

Dignity House...

In the large foyer The original staff from Pine Ridge Nursing Home are lined up standing at attention. The staff includes Biff, Jack, Nurse Ratchet, Nurse Ogle and Lou. Super Granny is standing in front of them, with a serious look on her face, giving them a lecture. "Now we won't have none of those shenanigans that we had at the other place. Residents are to be given only medication that they truly need and they will be monitored for side effects. Also all residents will be treated with dignity and respect. Anyone who does not comply with this will have to deal directly with me and you won't like it one bit."

Super Granny goes from very serious to very friendly. "Now who wants cookies?"

144

Biff timidly raises his hand. Everyone looks at him, Lou then raises his hand, Jack raises his hand. Then everyone raises their hands, Super Granny smiles proudly.

Now - Grace "Super Granny" Hudson - Dignity House Manager

Stephanie continues to tell Emily and Ethan about Dignity House. "We also have a great maintenance man who keeps everything in tip-top shape and safe."

Dignity House front porch...

Mr. Fix-it is putting the last nail in a new front porch railing, there is one post left. Mr. Fix-it grabs a post and an electric saw, he puts the saw on the post preparing to cut. He closes one eye and looks at the opening where the post will go, he adjusts the saw and makes the cut. He then stands the post up in place and it's a perfect fit, he smiles proudly, then winks at a near by resident, who's looking on.

Now - Dale "Mr. Fix-it" Spencer - Dignity House Maintenance Foreman

Stephanie continues. "We also have exercise classes to keep the residents fit and strong, you will love the instructor, she teaches fitness classes through the week and puts on wrestling exhibitions on the weekends."

Dignity House gym...
A large gym with exercise mats, weights and a boxing/wrestling ring. Wild Rose is in front of a group of seniors leading them through calisthenics. Wild Rose stops the calisthenics. Everyone is sweating and tired. "That was good folks now its time to hit the weights."
All the seniors looks at each other in shock.

The weekend...
In the ring, the Beast is laying on the mat apparently unconscious. Wild Rose is in the corner standing on the top rope holding her arms up. The crowd is roaring with cheer and coaxing her to jump. Wild Rose jumps from the top rope and slams hard on top of the beast and pins him to the mat. Stan steps into the ring with a microphone. "Its all over now lady's and gentlemen, another victory for the lovely, but tougher than steel Wild Rose."
Wild Rose stands and raises her fists above her head and the crowd goes wild.

Now- Rose "Wild Rose" Gibson - Dignity House Fitness Instructor and Professional Wrestler

Stephanie continues. "We also have various activities that the residents can take part in, one of which is horseback riding. The instructor is very experienced and a professional rider and all around cowboy. He gives riding lessons during the week and on weekends he puts on wild west shows."

Dignity House outdoor arena...

A large dirt arena with stadium seating all around it, the seats are empty. Cowboy is leading a horse while Marge rides it. "Your doing great Marge your a real natural, we'll have you barrel racing before you know it."

Marge bats eyes flirtatiously. "Oh Cowboy, your the best."

The weekend...

The stadium seating is now full with spectators cheering. Cowboy is in the ring, doing what he does best shooting and riding.

Now - Cecil "Cowboy" Poindexter - Dignity House Horse Riding Instructor, Wild West Performer and All Around Cowboy

Stephanie continues. "We also have excellent security the daytime security guard is an ex police officer and knows exactly what she's doing."

Dignity house visitor parking...

A graveled parking lot for visitors with several cars parked in it. Bean Pole, Skizz and Bonehead are sneaking around the cars. Lady Po Po now dressed in a pressed pristine security uniform and looking great, walks over to Bean Pole grabs him and throws him into Skizz and Bonehead, knocking them to the ground. "Don't even think about stealing anything around here, this place is off limits, don't let me catch you here again, now get."

All three Gang Bangers jump up and run away holding onto their pants so they don't fall down.

Now - Margret "Lady Po Po" Jefferson - Dignity House Head of Security Day Shift

Stephanie proudly continues describing the staff and services of Dignity House, as she fondly imagines each event. "We also have night security the man who handles that used to be an Army Ranger and he never fails a mission."

Dignity House side lawn...

Its dark out and the side of the house has hedges and bushes along the side of the wall. Bean Pole, Skizz and Bonehead are approaching with paint spray cans in their hands. Just as the three Gang Bangers get close to the house. G.I., dressed in black military fatigues, face paint and a watch cap, jumps out of the bushes yelling with a knife in his hand. "AAAAGGGHHH."

The three Gang Banger's eyes go wide with fear and they bolt as fast as they can go. G.I. sheaths his knife and has a good laugh. "I love this job."

Biff comes around the corner to see whats going on. G.I. looks up and spots him, he points two fingers to his own eyes then points at Biff. "I got my eyes on you too Daisy May."

Biff turns and runs off screaming like a little girl. G.I. smiles proudly, takes a cigar out of his pocket and puts it in his mouth. "Best job ever."

Now - Joe "G.I." Cotton - Dignity House Head of Security Night Shift

Stephanie continues as Emily and Ethan listen on intently. "We also have a grounds keeper that keeps the grounds spotless."

Dignity House front lawn...

Dirty Larry is picking up trash with a trash poker pole and putting it in an over the shoulder trash bag, he is now bathed, clean shaven, hair combed and dressed really neat looking proper and dandy, he whistles while picking up trash like he's really enjoying himself. He stabs an old half eaten candy bar and holds it up to look at it, he looks around in all directions to see if anyone is watching, then grabs the candy bar and sticks it in

149

his mouth. He smiles proudly as he chews like its tastes really great. "I think I might get used to this job thing."

Now - Larry "Dirty Larry" Westwood - Dignity House Grounds Keeper

Dignity House...

As Stephanie enthusiastically finishes telling about Dignity House, Ethan and Emily are pleased with the way Dignity House is run. "All the residents are treated like adults with dignity and honor no one is mistreated here. I think that just about covers it. How would you both like a tour?"

Ethan looks at Emily. Emily nods in agreement. "That would be great, we'd love to see the place, it sounds like a great place to live." Ethan says.

Stephanie smiles at Ethan and Emily then turns to address Cowboy. "Cowboy would you be kind enough to give the Trevors a tour?

Cowboy stands up and walks toward them and tugs on the front of his hat. "It'd be an honor ma'am."

Cowboy points to the hallway. "If you folks would come with me we'll start with the rooms."

The threesome head towards the hallway at one side of the foyer. "So Mr. Trevor what did ya do before ya retired?" Cowboy asks.

Ethan smiles."I was a Hollywood stuntman."

Cowboy smiles real big, pushes his hat up a bit and pats Ethan on the back. "Well Pard I reckon your gonna fit in around here just fine, just fine and dandy."

THE END